Aberdeenshire

COUNCIL

Aberdeenshire Libraries
www.aberdeenshire.gov.uk/libraries
Renewals Hotline 01224 661511

D1341993

3159369

"I am to decide your punishment for you," Mikael said finally.

"What are the choices?"

"Seven years' house arrest here in Haslam—"

"Seven *years*?"

"Or I take you as my wife."

"That's not funny. Not even remotely funny."

"It's not a joke. I either marry you, or leave you here in Haslam to begin your house arrest."

He saw Jemma recoil and her face turn white.

"I warned you that Sheikh Azizzi would not be lenient. He is not a Copeland fan either. He knows what your father did to my mother, and he wants to send a message that Saidia will not tolerate crime or immorality."

"But seven years!" She reached for the edge of the table to steady herself. "That's…that's…so long."

"Seven years or marriage," he corrected.

"No. *No*. Marriage isn't an option. I won't marry you. I would never marry you. I *could* never marry you."

THE DISGRACED COPELANDS

A family in the headlines—for all the wrong reasons!

For the Copeland family each day brings another tabloid scandal. Their world was one of unrivalled luxury and glittering social events. Now their privileged life is nothing but a distant memory…

Staring the taunting paparazzi straight in the eye, the Copeland heirs seek to start new lives— with no one to rely on but themselves. At least that's what they think…!

It seems fame and riches can't buy happiness— but they make it fun trying!

Read Morgan Copeland's story in:
The Fallen Greek Bride

Read Jemma Copeland's story in:
His Defiant Desert Queen

Look out for more scandalous stories about

The Disgraced Copelands

by Jane Porter

Coming soon!

HIS DEFIANT DESERT QUEEN

BY
JANE PORTER

MILLS BOON

First published in Great Britain 2015
by Mills & Boon, an imprint of Harlequin (UK) Limited,
Eton House, 18-24 Paradise Road, Richmond, Surrey, TW9 1SR

ISBN: 978-0-263-25755-7

Harlequin (UK) Limited's policy is to use papers that are natural, renewable and recyclable products and made from wood grown in sustainable forests. The logging and manufacturing processes conform to the legal environmental regulations of the country of origin.

Printed and bound in Great Britain
by CPI Antony Rowe, Chippenham, Wiltshire

New York Times and *USA TODAY* bestselling author **Jane Porter** has written forty romances and eleven women's fiction novels since her first sale to Mills & Boon® Modern™ Romance in 2000. A five-time RITA® finalist, Jane is known for her passionate, emotional and sensual novels, and loves nothing more than alpha heroes, exotic locations and happy-ever-afters. Today Jane lives in sunny San Clemente, California, with her surfer husband and three sons. Visit www.janeporter.com

Books by Jane Porter

The Disgraced Copelands
The Fallen Greek Bride

A Royal Scandal
His Majesty's Mistake
Not Fit for a King?

The Desert Kings
King of the Desert, Captive Bride
The Sheikh's Chosen Queen

Greek Tycoons
At the Greek Boss's Bidding

Ruthless
Hollywood Husband, Contract Wife

Desert Brides
The Sheikh's Disobedient Bride

A Dark Sicilian Secret
Duty, Desire and the Desert King

Visit the author profile page at
www.millsandboon.co.uk for more titles

For Lee Hyat,
who has been there every step of the way since reading
The Italian Groom! Thank you for being
my first reader and a most loyal and cherished friend.

PROLOGUE

SEETHING, SHEIKH MIKAEL KARIM, King of Saidia, watched the high fashion photo shoot taking place in the desert—his desert—wondering how anyone could think it was okay to enter a foreign country under a false identity and think he, or *she*, as it happened to be in this case, could get away with it.

Apparently the world was filled with fools.

Fools by the name of *Copeland.*

Jaw tight, temper barely leashed, Mikael waited for the right moment to intervene.

He'd been pushed too far, challenged directly, and he'd meet that challenge with swift retribution.

A king didn't negotiate. A king never begged, and a king refused to curry favor.

Saidia might be a small kingdom, but it was powerful. And the government of Saidia might tolerate the West, but Westerners couldn't enter Saidia, flaunt Saidia law, and think there would be no repercussions.

Jemma Copeland was a foolish woman. So like her father, thumbing her nose at the law, believing she was above it.

Perhaps Daniel Copeland had got away with his crimes. But his daughter would not be so lucky. Miss Jemma Copeland was going to pay.

CHAPTER ONE

NECESSITY HAD TAUGHT Jemma Copeland to shut out distractions.

She'd learned to ignore the things she didn't want to think about, to enable her to do what needed to be done.

So for the past two hours she'd ignored the scorching heat of the Sahara. The insistent, hollow ache in her stomach. The stigma of being a Copeland, and what it meant back home in the United States.

She'd blocked out heat, hunger, and shame, but she couldn't block out the tall, white-robed man standing just a foot behind the photographer, watching her through dark, unsmiling eyes while a half dozen robed men stood behind him.

She knew who the man was. How could she not? He'd attended her sister's wedding five years ago in Greenwich and every woman with a pulse had noticed Sheikh Mikael Karim. He was tall, he was impossibly, darkly handsome, and he was a billionaire as well as the new king of Saidia.

But Mikael Karim wasn't supposed to be on set today. He was supposed to be in Buenos Aires this week and his sudden appearance, arriving in a parade of glossy black luxury SUVs with tinted windows, had sent ripples of unease throughout the entire crew.

It was obvious he wasn't happy.

Jemma's gut told her something ugly could happen soon. She prayed she was wrong. She just wanted to get through the rest of the shoot and fly out tomorrow morning as planned.

At least he hadn't shown up yesterday. Yesterday had been

grueling, a very long day, with multiple shots in multiple locations, and the heat had been intense. But she hadn't complained. She wouldn't. She needed the job too much to be anything but grateful for the chance to still work.

It still boggled her mind how much things had changed. Just a year ago she had been one of America's golden girls, envied for her beauty, her wealth, her status as an It Girl. Her family was powerful, affluent. The Copelands had homes scattered across the world, and she and her gorgeous, privileged sisters were constantly photographed and discussed. But even the powerful can fall, and the Copeland family tumbled off their pedestal with the revelation that Daniel, her father, was the number two man in the biggest Ponzi scheme in America in the past century.

Overnight the Copelands became the most hated family in America.

Now Jemma could barely make ends meet. The fallout from her father's arrest, and the blitz of media interest surrounding the case, had destroyed her career. The fact that she worked, and had supported herself since she was eighteen, meant nothing to the public. She was still Daniel Copeland's daughter. Hated. Loathed. Resented.

Ridiculed.

Today, she was lucky to get work, and her once brilliant career now barely paid the bills. When her agency came to her with this assignment, a three day shoot with two travel days, meaning she'd be paid for five work days, she'd jumped at the opportunity to come to Saidia, the independent desert kingdom tucked underneath Southern Morocco, and nestled between the Western Sahara and the Atlantic Ocean. She'd continued to fight for the opportunity even when the Saidia consulate denied her visa request.

It wasn't legal, but desperate times called for desperate measures so she'd reapplied for a new visa as her sister, using Morgan's passport bearing Morgan's married name, Xanthos. This time she'd received the needed travel visa.

Yes, she was taking a huge risk, coming here under a false name, but she needed money. Without this paycheck, she wouldn't be able to pay her next month's mortgage.

So here she was, dressed in a long fox fur and thigh high boots, sweltering beneath the blazing sun.

So what if she was naked beneath the coat?

She was working. She was surviving. And one day, she'd thrive again, too.

So let them look.

Let them *all* look—the disapproving sheikh and his travel guard—because she wouldn't be crushed. She refused to be crushed. The clothes were beautiful. Life was exciting. She didn't have a care in the world.

Despite her fierce resolve, perspiration beaded beneath her full breasts and slid down her bare abdomen.

Not uncomfortable, she thought. *Sexy.*

And with sexy firmly in mind, she drew a breath, jutted her hip, and struck a bold pose.

Keith, the Australian photographer, let out an appreciative whistle. "That's beautiful, baby! More of that, please."

She felt a rush of pleasure, which was quickly dashed by the sight of Mikael Karim moving closer to Keith.

The sheikh was tall, so tall he towered over Keith, and his shoulders were broad, dwarfing the slender Australian.

Jemma had forgotten just how intensely handsome Mikael Karim was. She'd modeled in other countries and had met many different sheikhs, and most had been short, heavyset men with flirty eyes and thickening jowls.

But Sheikh Mikael Karim was young, and lean, and fierce. His white robes only accentuated the width of his shoulders as well as his height, and his angular jaw jutted, black eyebrows flat over those intense, dark eyes.

Now Sheikh Karim looked over Keith's head, his dark gaze piercing her, holding her attention. She couldn't look away. He seemed to be telling her something, warning her of something. She went hot, then cold, shivering despite the heat.

Her stomach rose, fell. An alarm sounded in her head. He was dangerous.

She tugged on the edges of the coat, pulling it closer to her body, suddenly very conscious of the fact that she was naked beneath.

Sighing with frustration, Keith lowered his camera a fraction. "You just lost all your energy. Give me sexy, baby."

Jemma glanced at the sheikh from beneath her lashes. The man oozed tension, a lethal tension that made her legs turn to jelly and the hair prickle on the back of her neck. Something was wrong. Something was very wrong.

But Keith couldn't read Sheikh Karim's expression and his irritation grew. "Come on, focus. We need to wrap this up, baby."

Keith was right. They did need to wrap this shot. And she was here to do a job. She had to deliver, or she'd never work again.

Jemma gulped a breath, squared her shoulders, and lifted her chin to the sun, feeling her long hair spill down her back as she let the heavy fur drop off her shoulder, exposing more skin.

"Nice." Keith lifted his camera, motioned for his assistant to step closer with the white reflective screen, and began snapping away. "I like that. More of that."

Jemma shook her head, letting her thick hair tease the small of her spine even as the fur fell lower on her breasts.

"Perfect," Keith crooned. "That's hot. Love it. Don't stop. You're on fire now."

Yes, she was, she thought, arching her shoulders back, breasts thrust high, the nipples now just exposed to the kiss of the sun. In Sheikh Karim's world she was probably going to burn in the flames of hell, but there was nothing she could do about it. This was her job. She had to deliver. And so she pushed all other thoughts from mind, except for giving the image they wanted.

Her shoulders twisted and the coat slid lower on her arm, the fur tickling the back of her bare thighs.

"Lovely, baby." Keith was snapping away. "So beautiful. Keep doing what you're doing. You're a goddess. Every man's dream."

She wasn't a goddess, or a dream, but she could pretend to be. She could pretend anything for a short period of time. Pretending gave her distance, allowing her to breathe, escape, escaping the reality of what was happening at home. *Home.* A sinking sensation filled her. *What a nightmare.*

Battling back the sadness, Jemma shifted, lifting her chin, thrusting her hip out, dropping the coat altogether, exposing her breasts, nipples jutting proudly.

Keith whistled softly. "Give me more."

"*No,*" Sheikh Mikael Karim ground out. It was just one word, but it echoed like a crack of thunder, immediately silencing the murmur of stylists, make-up artist, and lighting assistants.

All heads turned toward the sheikh.

Jemma stared at him, her stomach churning all over again.

The sheikh's expression was beyond fierce. His lips curled, his dark eyes burned as he pushed the camera in Keith's hands down. "That's enough," he gritted. "I've had enough, from all of you." His narrowed gaze swept the tents and crew. "You are done here."

And then his head turned again and he stared straight at Jemma. "And you, Miss *Copeland.* Cover yourself, and then go inside the tent. I will be in to deal with you shortly."

She covered herself, but didn't move.

The sheikh had called her *Miss Copeland,* not Mrs. Xanthis, the name she'd used on the visa, but Copeland.

Panic flooded her veins. Her heart surged. Sheikh Karim knew who she was. He'd recognized her after all these years. The realization shocked her. He, who knew so many, remembered her.

Hands shaking, she tugged the coat closer to her body, suddenly icy cold despite the dazzling heat. "What's happening?" she whispered, even though in a dim part of her brain, she knew.

She'd been found out. Her true identity had been discovered. How, she didn't know, but she was in trouble. Grave trouble. She could feel the severity of the situation all the way down to her toes.

"I think you know," Sheikh Karim said flatly. "Now go inside the tent and wait."

Her knees knocked. She wasn't sure her legs could support her. "For what?"

"To be informed of the charges being brought against you."

"I've done nothing wrong."

His dark eyes narrowed. His jaw hardened as his gaze swept over her, from the top of her head to the boots on her feet. "You've done *everything* wrong, Miss *Copeland*. You're in serious trouble. So go to the tent, now, and if you have half a brain, you'll obey."

Jemma had more than half a brain. She actually had a very good brain. And a very good imagination, which made the walk to the tent excruciating.

What was going to happen to her? What were the official charges? And what would the punishment be?

She tried to calm herself. She focused on her breathing, and clamped down on her wild thoughts. It wouldn't help her to panic. She knew she'd entered the country illegally. She'd willingly agreed to work on a shoot that hadn't been condoned by the government. *And* she'd shown her breasts in public, which was also against Saidia's law.

And she'd done it all because she hadn't taken money from her family since she was eighteen and she wasn't about to start now.

She was an adult. A successful, capable woman. And she'd been determined to make it without going to her family begging for a handout.

In hindsight, perhaps begging for a handout would have been wiser.

In the wardrobe tent, Jemma shrugged off the heavy fur coat, and slipped a light pink cotton kimono over her shoulders, tying the sash at her waist. As she sat down at the stool before the make-up mirror, she could hear the sheikh's voice echo in her head.

You've done everything wrong...

Everything wrong...

He was right. She had done everything wrong. She prayed he'd accept her apology, allow her to make amends. She hadn't meant to insult him, or disrespect his country or his culture in any way.

Jemma straightened, hearing voices outside her tent. The voices were pitched low, speaking quickly, urgently. Male voices. A single female voice. Jemma recognized the woman as Mary Leed, *Catwalk*'s editorial director. Mary was usually unflappable but she sounded absolutely panicked now.

Jemma's heart fell all over again. Bad. This was bad.

She swallowed hard, her stomach churning, nerves threatening to get the better of her.

She shouldn't have come.

She shouldn't have taken such risks.

But what was she to do otherwise? Crumble? Shatter? End up on the streets, destitute, homeless, helpless?

No.

She wouldn't be helpless, and she wouldn't be pitied, or mocked, either.

She'd suffered enough at the hands of her father. He'd betrayed them all; his clients, his business partners, his friends, even his family. He might be selfish and ruthless and destructive, but the rest of the Copelands weren't. Copelands were good people.

Good people, she silently insisted, stretching out one leg to unzip the thigh-high boot. Her hand was trembling so badly that it made it difficult to get the zipper down. The boots were outrageous to start with. They were the stuff of fantasy, a very high heel projecting a kinky twist, just like the fashion layout itself.

They would have been smarter doing this feature in Palm Springs instead of Saidia with Saidia's strict laws of moral conduct. Saidia might be stable and tolerant, but it wasn't a democracy, nor did it cater to the wealthy Westerners like some other nations. It remained conservative and up until two generations ago, marriages weren't just arranged, they were forced.

The tribal leaders kidnapped their brides from neighboring tribes.

Unthinkable to the modern Western mind, but acceptable here.

Jemma was tugging the zipper down on the second boot when the tent flap parted and Mary entered with Sheikh Karim. Two members of the sheikh's guard stood at the entrance.

Jemma slowly sat up, and looked from Mary to the sheikh and back.

Mary's face was pale, her lips pressed thin. "We've a problem," she said.

Silence followed. Jemma curled her fingers into her lap.

Mary wouldn't meet Jemma's gaze, looking past her shoulder instead. "We're wrapping up the shoot and returning to the capitol immediately. We are facing some legal charges and fines, which we are hoping to take care of quickly so the crew and company can return to England tomorrow, or the next day." She hesitated for a long moment, before adding even more quietly, "At least most of us should be able to return to England tomorrow or the next day. Jemma, I'm afraid you won't be going with us."

Jemma started to rise, but remembered her boot and sat back down. "Why not?"

"The charges against you are different," Mary said, still avoiding Jemma's gaze. "We are in trouble for using you, but you, you're in trouble for…" Her voice faded away. She didn't finish the sentence.

She didn't have to.

Jemma knew why she was in trouble. What she didn't know was what she'd be charged with. "I'm sorry." She drew a quick, shallow breath and looked from Mary to Sheikh Karim. "I am sorry. Truly—"

"Not interested," he said curtly.

Jemma's stomach flipped. "I made a mistake—"

"A mistake is pairing a black shoe and a blue shoe. A mistake is forgetting to charge one's phone. A mistake is *not* entering the country illegally, under false pretenses, with a false identity. You had no work permit. No visa. Nothing." Sheikh Karim's voice crackled with contempt and fury. "What you did was deliberate, and a felony, Miss Copeland."

Jemma put a hand to her belly, praying she wouldn't throw up here, now. She hadn't eaten much today. She never did on days she worked, knowing she photographed better with a very flat stomach. "What can I do to make this right?"

Mary shot Sheikh Karim a stricken glance.

He shook his head, once. "There is nothing. The magazine staff must appear in court, and pay their fines. You will face a different judge, and be sentenced accordingly."

Jemma sat very still. "So I'm to be separated from everyone?"

"Yes." The sheikh gestured to Mary. "You and the rest of the crew, are to leave immediately. My men will accompany you to ensure your safety." He glanced at Jemma. "And you will come with me."

Mary nodded and left. Heart thudding, Jemma watched Mary's silent, abrupt departure then looked to Sheikh Karim.

He was angry. Very, very angry.

Three years ago she might have crumbled. Two years ago she might have cried. But that was the old Jemma, the girl who'd grown up pampered, protected by a big brother and three opinionated, but loving, sisters.

She wasn't that girl anymore. In fact, she wasn't a girl at all anymore. She'd been put to the fire and she'd come out fierce. Strong.

"So where *do* felons go, Sheikh Karim?" she asked quietly, meeting the sheikh's hard narrowed gaze.

"To prison."

"I'm going to prison?"

"If you were to go to court tomorrow, and appear before our judicial tribunal, yes. But you're not being seen by our judicial tribunal. You're being seen by my tribe's elder, and he will act as judge."

"Why a different court and judge than Mary and the magazine crew?"

"Because they are charged with crimes against Saidia. You—" he broke off, studying her lovely face in the mirror, wondering how she'd react to his news, "You are charged with crimes against the Karims, my family. Saidia's royal family. You will be escorted to a judge who is of my tribe. He will hear the charges brought against you, and then pass judgment."

She didn't say anything. Her brow creased and she looked utterly bewildered. "I don't understand. What have I done to your family?"

"You stole from my family. Shamed them."

"But I haven't. I don't even know your family."

"Your father does."

Jemma grew still. Everything seemed to slow, stop. Would the trail of devastation left by her father's action never end? She stared at Mikael suddenly afraid of what he'd say next. "But I'm not my father."

"Not physically, no, but you represent him."

"I don't."

"You do." His jaw hardened. "In Arabic society, one is always connected to one's family. You represent your family throughout your life, which is why it's so important to always bring honor to one's family. But your father stole from the

Karims, shamed the Karims, dishonoring my family, and in so doing, he dishonored all of Saidia."

She swallowed hard. "But I'm nothing like my father."

"You are his daughter, and you are here, unlawfully. It is time to right the wrong. You will make atonement for your disrespect, and your father's, too."

"I don't even have a relationship with my father. I haven't seen him in years—"

"This is not the time. We have a long trip ahead of us. I suggest you finish changing so we can get on the road."

Her fingers bent, nails pressing to the dressing table. *"Please."*

"It's not up to me."

"But you are the king."

"And kings must insist on obedience, submission, and respect. Even from our foreign visitors."

She looked at him, seeing him, but not seeing him, too overwhelmed by his words and the implication of what he was saying to focus on any one thing. It didn't help that her pulse raced, making her head feel dizzy and light.

The grim security guard at Tagadir International Airport had warned them. Had said that His Highness Sheikh Karim was all powerful in Saidia. As king he owned this massive expanse of desert and the sand dunes rolling in every direction, and as their translator had whispered on leaving the airport, *"His Highness, Sheikh Karim, isn't just head of the country, he is the country."*

Jemma exhaled slowly, trying to clear the fog and panic from her brain. She should have taken the warnings seriously. She should have been logical, not desperate.

Desperate was a dangerous state of mind.

Desperate fueled chaos.

What she needed to do was remain calm. Think this through. There had to be a way to reach him, reason with him. Surely he didn't make a habit of locking up American and British girls?

"I'd like to make amends," she said quietly, glancing up at Sheikh Karim from beneath her lashes, taking in his height, the width of his shoulders, and his hard, chiseled features. Nothing in his expression was kind. There was not even a hint of softness at his mouth.

"You will," he said. "You must."

She winced at the harshness in his voice. Sheikh Mikael Karim might be as handsome as any Hollywood leading man, but there was no warmth in his eyes.

He was a cold man, and she knew all too well that cold men were dangerous. Men without hearts destroyed, and if she were not very careful, and very smart, she could be ruined.

"Can I pay a fine? A penalty?"

"You're in no position to buy yourself out of trouble, Miss Copeland. Your family is bankrupt."

"I could try Drakon—"

"You're not calling anyone," he interrupted sharply. "And I won't have Drakon bailing you out. He might be your sister's ex-husband, but he was my friend from university and from what I understand, he lost virtually his entire fortune thanks to your father. I think Drakon has paid a high enough price for being associated with you Copelands. It's time you and your family stopped expecting others to clean up your messes and instead assumed responsibility for your mistakes."

"That might be, but Drakon isn't cruel. He wouldn't approve of you…of you…" Her voice failed her as she met Mikael's dark gaze. The sheikh's anger burned in his eyes, scorching her.

"Of what, Miss Copeland?" he asked softly, a hint of menace in his deep voice.

"What won't he approve of?" he persisted.

Jemma couldn't answer. Her heart beat wildly, a painful staccato that made her chest ache.

She had to be careful. She couldn't afford to alienate the sheikh. Not when she needed him and his protection.

She needed to win him over. She needed him to care. Somehow she had to get him to see her, the real her, *Jemma*. The person. The woman. Not the daughter of Daniel Copeland.

It was vital she didn't antagonize him, but reached him. Otherwise it would be far too easy for Sheikh Karim to snap his fingers and destroy her. He was that powerful, that ruthless.

Her eyes burned and her lip trembled and she bit down hard, teeth digging into her lip to keep from making a sound.

Fear washed through her but she would not crack, or cry. Would not disintegrate, either.

"He wouldn't approve of me flaunting your laws," she said lowly, fighting to maintain control, and cling to whatever dignity she had left. "He wouldn't approve of me using my sister's passport, either. He would be angry," she added, lifting her chin to meet Sheikh Karim's gaze. "And disappointed."

Mikael Karim arched a brow.

"In me," she added. "He'd be disappointed in me."

And then wrapping herself in courage, and hanging on to that fragile cloak, she removed her boot, placing it on the floor next to its mate, and turned to her dressing table to begin removing her make-up.

CHAPTER TWO

MIKAEL SAW JEMMA'S lower lip quiver before she clamped her jaw, biting down in an effort to remain silent, as she turned back to her dressing table.

He was surprised at how calm she was. He'd expected tears. Hysteria. Instead she was quiet. Thoughtful. Respectful.

He'd planned on defiance. He'd come prepared for theatrics. She'd almost gone there. Almost, but then thought better of it.

Perhaps she wasn't as silly as he'd thought.

Perhaps she might have a brain in her pretty head after all.

He was glad she wasn't going to dissolve into tears and hysteria. And glad she might be starting to understand the gravity of her situation.

But even then, he was still deeply furious with her for knowingly, willfully flaunting every international law by entering a foreign country with a false identity, and then practically stripping in public.

It wasn't done.

It wasn't acceptable.

It wouldn't even be allowed in San Francisco or New York City.

So how could she think it would be okay here?

His brow lowered as his narrowed gaze swept over her. She looked so soft and contrite now as she removed her makeup. It was an act. He was certain she was playing him. Just as her father had played his mother...before bankrupting her, breaking her.

His mother would be alive today if Daniel Copeland hadn't lied to her and stolen from her, taking not just her financial security, but her self-respect.

Thank goodness Mikael was not his mother.

He knew better than to allow himself to be manipulated by yet another Copeland con artist.

Mikael refused to pity Jemma. He didn't care if she was sorry. Had Daniel Copeland shown his mother mercy? No. Had Daniel Copeland shown any of his clients concern…compassion? *No.* So why should his daughter receive preferential treatment?

"Will I have a lawyer present?" she asked, breaking the silence.

"No," he said.

"Will I have any legal representation?"

"No."

She hesitated, brow furrowing, lips compressing, somehow even more lovely troubled than when posed on the desert sand in the fur and thigh high boots.

Yes, she was beautiful. And yes, she'd inherited her mother's famous bone structure, and yes, even in this dim, stifling tent she still glowed like a jewel—glossy dark hair, brilliant green eyes, luminous skin, pink lips—but that didn't change the fact that she was a criminal.

"Neither of us have lawyers," he added, hating that he was even aware of her beauty. He shouldn't notice, or care. He shouldn't feel any attraction at all. "There is just the case itself, presented by me, and then the judge passes the sentence."

"You represent yourself?"

"I represent my tribe, the Karim family, and the laws of this country."

She turned slowly on the stool to face him, her hands resting on her thighs, the pink kimono gaping slightly above the knotted sash, revealing the slope of her full breast. "What you're saying is that it will be you testifying against me."

He shouldn't know that her nipple was small and pink and that her belly was flat above firm, rounded hips.

Or at the very least, he shouldn't remember. He shouldn't want to remember. "I present the facts. I do not pass judgment."

"Will the *facts* be presented in English?"

"No."

"So you could say anything."

"But why would I?" he countered sharply. "You've broken numerous laws. Important laws. Laws created to protect our borders and the safety and security of my people. There is no need to add weight or severity. What you've done is quite serious. The punishment will be appropriately serious."

He saw a flash in her eyes, and he didn't know if it was anger or fear but she didn't speak. She bit down, holding back the quick retort.

Seconds ticked by, one after the other.

For almost a minute there was only silence, a tense silence weighted with all the words she refrained from speaking.

"How serious?" she finally asked.

"There will be jail time."

"How long?"

He was uncomfortable with all the questions. "Do you really want to do this now?"

"Absolutely. Far better to be prepared than to walk in blind."

"The minimum sentence is somewhere between five to ten years. The maximum, upward of twenty."

She went white, and her lips parted, but she made no sound. She simply stared at him, incredulous, before slowly turning back to face her dressing table mirror.

She was trying not to cry.

Her shoulders were straight, and her head was high but he saw the welling of tears in her eyes. He felt her shock, and sadness.

He should leave but his feet wouldn't move. His chest felt tight.

It was her own damned fault.

But he could still see her five years ago in the periwinkle blue bridesmaid dress at Morgan's wedding.

He could hear her gurgle of laughter as she'd made a toast to her big sister at the reception after.

"We will leave as soon as you're dressed," he said tersely, ignoring Jemma's pallor and the trembling of her hands where they rested on the dressing table.

"I will need five or ten minutes," she said.

"Of course." He turned to leave but from the corner of his eye he saw her lean toward the mirror to try to remove the strip of false eyelashes on her right eye, her hands still shaking so much she couldn't lift the edge.

It wasn't his problem. He didn't care if her hands shook violently or not. But he couldn't stop watching her. He couldn't help noticing that she was struggling. Tears spilled from the corners of her eyes as she battled to get the eyelashes off.

It was her fault.

He wasn't responsible for her situation.

And yet her struggle unsettled him, awakening emotions and memories he didn't want to feel.

Mikael didn't believe in feeling. Feelings were best left to others. He, on the other hand, preferred logic. Structure. Rules. Order.

He wouldn't be moved by tears. Not even the tears of a young foreign woman that he'd met many years ago at the wedding of Drakon Xanthis, his close friend from university. Just because Drakon had married Jemma's older sister, Morgan, didn't mean that Mikael had to make allowances. Why make allowances when Daniel Copeland had made none for his mother?

"Stop," he ordered, unable to watch her struggle any longer. "You're about to take out your eye."

"I have to get them off."

"Not like that."

"I can do it."

"You're making a mess of it." He crossed the distance, gestured for her to turn on her stool. "Face me, and hold still. Look down. Don't move."

Jemma held her breath as she felt his fingers against her temple. His touch was warm, his hand steady as he used the tip of his finger to lift the edge of the strip and then he slowly, carefully peeled the lashes from her lid. "One down," he said, putting the crescent of lashes in her hand. "One to go."

He made quick work on the second set.

"You've done this before," she said, as he took a step back, putting distance between them, but not enough distance. He was so big, so intimidating, that she found his nearness overwhelming.

"I haven't, but I've watched enough girlfriends put on make up to know how it's done."

She looked at him for a long moment, her gaze searching his. "And you have *no* say in the sentencing?" she asked.

"I have plenty of say," he answered. "I am the king. I can make new laws, pass laws, break laws…but breaking laws wouldn't make me a good king or a proper leader for my people. So I, too, observe the laws of Saidia, and am committed to upholding them."

"Could you ask the judge to be lenient with me?"

"I could."

"But you won't?"

He didn't answer right away, which was telling, she thought.

"Would you ask for leniency for another woman?"

His broad shoulders shifted. "It would depend on who she was, and what she'd done."

"So your relationship with her would influence your decision?"

"Absolutely."

"I see."

"As her *character* would influence my decision."

And he didn't approve of her character.

Jemma understood then that he wouldn't help her in any way. He didn't like her. He didn't approve of her. And he felt no pity or compassion because she was a Copeland and it was a Copeland, her father, who had wronged his family.

In his mind, she had so many strikes against her she wasn't worth saving.

For a moment she couldn't breathe. The pain was so sharp and hard it cut her to the quick.

It was almost like the pain when Damien ended their engagement. He'd said he'd loved her. He'd said he wanted to spend his life with her. But then when he began losing jobs, he backed away from her. Far better to lose her, than his career.

Throat aching, eyes burning, Jemma turned back to the mirror.

She reached for a brush and ran it slowly through her long dark hair, making the glossy waves ripple down her back, telling herself not to think, not to feel, and most definitely, not to cry.

"You expect your tribal elder to sentence me to prison, for at least five years?" she asked, drawing the brush through her long hair.

Silence stretched. After a long moment, Sheikh Karim answered, "I don't expect Sheikh Azizzi to give you a minimum sentence, no."

She nodded once. "Thank you for at least being honest."

And then she reached for the bottle of make-up remover and a cotton ball to remove what was left of her eye make-up.

He walked out then. Thank goodness. She'd barely kept it together there, at the end.

She was scared, so scared.

Would she really be going to prison?

Would he really allow the judge to have her locked away for years?

She couldn't believe this was happening. Had to be a bad dream. But the sweltering heat inside the tent felt far too real to be a dream.

Jemma left her make-up table and went to her purse to retrieve her phone. Mary had informed the crew this morning as they left the hotel that they'd get no signal here in the desert, and checking her phone now she saw that Mary was right. She couldn't call anyone. Couldn't alert anyone to her situation. As Jemma put her phone away, she could only pray that Mary would make some calls on her behalf once she returned to London.

Jemma changed quickly into her street clothes, a gray short linen skirt, white knit top and gray blazer.

Drawing a breath, she left the tent, stepping out into the last lingering ray of light. Two of the sheikh's men guarded the tent, but they didn't acknowledge her.

The desert glowed with amber, ruby and golden colors. The convoy of cars that had descended on the shoot two hours ago was half the number it'd been when Jemma had disappeared into the tent.

Sheikh Karim stepped from the back of one of the black vehicles. He gestured to her. "Come. We leave now."

She shouldered her purse, pretending the sheikh wasn't watching her walk toward him, pretending his guards weren't there behind her, watching her walk away from them. She pretended she was strong and calm, that nothing threatened her.

It was all she'd been doing since her father's downfall.

Pretending. Faking. Fighting.

"Ready?" Sheikh Karim asked as she reached his side.

"Yes."

"You have no suitcase, no clothes?"

"I have a few traveling pieces here, but the rest is in my suitcase." She clasped her oversized purse closer to her body. "Can we go get my luggage?"

"No."

"Will you send for it?"

"You won't need it where you are going."

Her eyes widened and her lips parted to protest but his grim expression silenced her.

He held open the door. The car was already running.

"It's time to go," he said firmly.

Swallowing, Jemma slid onto the black leather seat, terrified to leave this scorching desert, not knowing where she'd
go next.

Sheikh Karim joined her on the seat, his large body filling the back of the car. Jemma scooted as far over as she
could before settling her blazer over her thighs, hiding her
bare skin. But even sitting near the door, he was far too close,
and warm, so warm that she fixed her attention on the desert
beyond the car window determined to block out everything
until she was calm.

She stared hard at the landscape, imagining that she was
someone else, somewhere else and it soothed her. The sun
was lower in the sky and the colors were changing, darken-
ing, deepening and it made her heart hurt. In any other situation she would've been overcome by the beauty of the sunset.
As it was now, she felt bereft.

She'd come to Saidia to save what was left of her world,
and instead she'd shattered it completely.

The car was moving. Her stomach lurched. She gripped the
handle on the door and drew a deep breath and then another
to calm herself.

It was going to be okay.
Everything would be okay.
Everything would be fine.

"It's beautiful," she whispered, blinking back tears.

He said nothing.

She blinked again, clearing her vision, determined to find
her center…a place of peace, and calm. She had to keep her
head. There was no other way she'd survive whatever came
next if she didn't stay focused.

"Where does this elder, Sheikh Azizzi, live?" she asked,
keeping her gaze fixed on a distant dune. The sun was dropping more quickly, painting the sky a wash of rose and red that
reflected crimson against the sand.

"Haslam," he said.

"Is it far?"

"Two hours by car. If there is no sandstorm."

"Do you expect one?" she asked, glancing briefly in his direction.

"Not tonight, but it's not unusual as you approach the mountains. The wind races through the valley and whips the sand dunes. It's impressive if you're not trying to drive through, and maddening if you are."

He sounded so cavalier. She wondered just how dangerous a sandstorm really was. "The storm won't hurt us?"

The sheikh shrugged. "Not if we stay on the road, turn off the engine and close the vents. But I don't expect a sandstorm tonight. So far there appears to be little wind. I think it will be a quiet night in the desert."

She tried to picture the still crimson desert as a whirling sea of sand. She'd seen it in movies, but it seemed impossible now. "And so when do we see the judge?"

"Tonight."

"Tonight?" she echoed, and when he nodded, she added, "But we won't be there for hours."

"We are expected."

His answer unleashed a thousand butterflies inside her middle. "And will we know his verdict tonight?"

"Yes." Sheikh Karim's jaw hardened. "It will be a long night."

"Justice moves swiftly in Saidia," she said under her breath.

"You have no one to blame but yourself."

She flinched at his harsh tone, and held her tongue.

But the sheikh wasn't satisfied with her silence. "Why did you do it?" he demanded, his voice almost savage. "You've had a successful career. Surely you could have been happy with less?"

"I'm broke. I needed the work. I would have lost my flat."

"You'll lose it anyway, now. There is no way for you to pay bills from prison."

She hadn't thought that far. She gave her head a bemused shake. "Maybe someone will be able to—" she broke off as she saw his expression. "Yes, I know. You don't think I deserve help, but you're wrong. I'm not who you think I am. I'm not this selfish, horrible woman you make me out to be."

"Then why did you enter Saidia with your sister's passport? I can't imagine she gave her passport to you."

"She didn't."

"I didn't think so," he ground out.

Jemma bit down on the inside of her lip, chewing her lip to keep from making a sound.

"I *know* Morgan," he added ruthlessly. "Drakon was one of my best friends. And you probably don't remember, or were too young to notice, but I attended Morgan and Drakon's wedding five years ago in Greenwich. Yes, you and Morgan might both be brunettes, but you don't look anything alike. It was beyond stupid to try to pass yourself off as her."

Fatigue and fear and dread made her heartsick, and his words drilled into her, like a hammer in her head, making her headache feel worse. She pressed her fingers to her temple to ease the pain. "How did you find out I was here?"

He shot her a cool look. "You had a very chatty stylist on the shoot. She sat in a bar two nights ago drinking and talking about the layout, the models, and you. Apparently your name was mentioned oh…a dozen times. *Jemma Copeland. That Jemma Copeland. Jemma Copeland, daughter of Daniel Copeland.* In today's age of technology and social media, it just took a couple Tweets and it went viral. One minute I was in Buenos Aires, thinking everything was fine at home, and then the next I was boarding my jet to return home to deal with *you.*"

He shifted, extending his long legs out, and she sucked in an uneasy breath. He was so big, and his legs were so long, she felt positively suffocated, trapped here in the back of the car with him.

"I wish you had just let me go. We were leaving tomorrow morning anyway," she said softly. "You were out of the country. You didn't have to rush home to have me arrested."

"No. I could have allowed the police to come for you. They were going to arrest you. They wouldn't have been as polite, or patient, as I've been. They would have handcuffed you and put you in the back of an armored truck and taken you to a jail where you'd languish for a few days, maybe a week, until you were seen by our tribunal, and then you would have been sentenced to five, ten, fifteen years…or longer…in our state run prison. It wouldn't have been pleasant. It wouldn't have been nice at all." His expression was fierce, his gaze held hers, critical, condemning. "You don't realize it, but I've done you a favor. I have intervened on your behalf, and yes, you will still serve time, but it will be in a smaller place, in a private home. My assistance allows you to serve your time under house arrest rather than a large state run prison. So you can thank your stars I found out."

"I'm amazed you'd intervene since you hate the Copelands so much."

His dark gaze met hers. "So am I."

CHAPTER THREE

For several minutes they traveled in silence.

"So why *did* you rush home from Buenos Aires since you despise the Copelands?" she asked, unable to stifle the question, genuinely curious about his motives.

He didn't answer immediately, and when he did, his answer was short, brusque. "Drakon."

She picked her next words with care. "You must know he won't approve of you locking me up, for six months or six years. I'm his sister-in-law."

"His ex-sister-in-law. Morgan and Drakon are divorced, or separated, or something of that nature."

"But he likes me. He has a soft spot for me."

Mikael's lips compressed. "Perhaps, but you're a felon. Even as protective as he is, he will still have to come to terms with the fact that you broke the law, and there are consequences. There must be consequences. Saidia cannot be lawless. Nor can I govern at whim." His head turned, and his dark eyes met hers. For a long moment there was just silence, and then he shrugged. "And at last, the Copelands will be held accountable for their crimes."

Her stomach flipped. Her heart lurched. "You want to see me suffer," she whispered.

"Your father should have accepted responsibility and answered for his actions. Instead he ran away."

"I hate what he did, Sheikh Karim. I hate that he betrayed his customers and clients...friends. His choices sicken me—"

"There was a reason your visa was denied. The refusal was a warning. The refusal should have protected you. You should not have come."

She turned her head and swiftly wiped away tears before they could fall.

No, she shouldn't have come to Saidia. She shouldn't have broken laws.

But she had.

And now she'd pay. And pay dearly.

She felt Mikael's gaze. She knew he was watching her. His close, critical scrutiny made her pulse race. She felt cornered. Trapped.

She hated the feeling. It was suffocating. Jemma's fingers wrapped around the door handle and gripped it tight. If only she could jump from the car. Fling herself into the desert. Hide. Disappear.

But of course it wouldn't work like that.

Her father had tried to evade arrest and he'd taken off in his yacht, setting across the ocean in hopes of finding some bit of paradise somewhere.

Instead his yacht had been commandeered off the coast of Africa and he'd been taken hostage and held for ransom. No one had paid. He'd been hostage for months now and the public loved it. They loved his shame and pain.

Jemma flinched and pressed her hands together, fingers lacing. She didn't like thinking about him, and especially didn't like to think of him helpless in some African coastal village.

If only he hadn't run.

If only he hadn't stolen his clients' money.

If only...

"The doors are locked," Mikael said flatly. "There is no escape."

Her eyes burned. She swallowed around the lump in her throat. "No," she murmured, "there isn't, is there?"

She turned her head away again, trembling inwardly. It had been such a bad, bad year. She still felt wrecked. Trashed. Devastated by her father's duplicity and deceit. And then heart-broken by Damien's rejection.

To have your own father destroy so many people's lives, and then to have the love of your life abruptly cast you off...

She couldn't have imagined that her life would derail so completely. One day everything was normal and then the next, absolute chaos and mayhem.

The media had converged on her immediately in London, camping outside her flat, the journalists three rows deep, each with cameras and microphones and questions they shouted at her every time she opened her front door.

"Jemma, how does it feel to know that your father is one of the biggest con artists in American history?"

"Do you or your family have any plans to pay all these bankrupt people back?"

"Where is all the money, Jemma?"

"Did your father use stolen money to pay for this flat?"

It had been difficult enduring the constant barrage of questions, but she came and went, determined to work, to keep life as normal as possible.

But within a week, the jobs disappeared.

She was no longer just Jemma, the face of Farrinelli, but that American, that Jemma *Copeland.*

Every major magazine and fashion house she'd been booked to work for had cancelled on her in quick succession.

It was bad enough that six months of work was lost, but then Damien had started losing jobs, too.

Damien couldn't get work.

Farrinelli cancelled Jemma's contract as the face of Farrinelli Fragrance. Damien didn't wait for Farrinelli to replace him too. He left Jemma, their flat, their life.

Jemma understood. She was bad for his career. Bad for business. For Damien. Farrinelli. Everyone.

Heartsick, miserable, she opened her eyes to discover Sheikh Karim watching her.

Tears filled her eyes. She was ashamed of the tears, ashamed for being weak. How could she cry or feel sorry for herself? She was better off than most people. Certainly better off than the thousands of people her father had impoverished.

But she never spoke about her father, or what he did. She didn't openly acknowledge the shame, either. There were no words for it. No way to ever make amends, either.

"Please don't think this is a challenge, nor is it meant to be disrespectful," she said quietly, swiftly dashing away tears before they could fall. "But I did not come here on a lark. I am not a rebel schoolgirl. I came to Saidia because I desperately needed the work. I had thought I'd fly in, work, fly out, and no one would be the wiser. Clearly, I was wrong, and for that, I am very sorry."

Mikael listened to the apology in silence. The apology meant nothing to him. Words were easy. They slipped from the tongue and lips with ease.

Actions, now those were difficult.

Action, and consequence, those required effort. Pain. Sweat. Sacrifice.

It crossed his mind that Jemma had no idea what was coming once they reached Haslam. Sheikh Azizzi, the judge, was not a soft touch. Sheikh Azizzi was old world, old school, and determined to preserve as much of the tribal customs as possible.

He was also Mikael's godfather and intimate with Karim family history, including Mikael's parents' drawn-out divorce, and his mother's subsequent banishment from Saidia.

Sheikh Azizzi had not been a fan of his mother, but the divorce had horrified Sheikh Azizzi and all of the country. Divorce was rare in Saidia, and in a thousand years of Karim rule, there had never been a divorce in the Karim royal family, and the drama and the endless publicity around it—the news in the international papers, not Saidia's—had alienated the Saidia public.

No, Mikael's father had not been a good king. If he hadn't died when he did, there might have been an uprising.

There *would* have been an uprising.

Which is why ever since Mikael had inherited the throne, he'd vowed to be a true leader to the Saidia people. A good king. A fair king. He'd vowed to represent his country properly, and he'd promised to protect the desert kingdom's culture, and preserve ancient Saidia customs.

Thus, the trip to Haslam to see Sheikh Azizzi.

Sheikh Azizzi was both a political and spiritual figure. He was a simple man, a village elder, but brave and wise. He and Mikael's father had grown up together, both from the same village. Sheikh Azizzi's father has served as a counselor and advisor to the royal Karim family, but Sheikh Azizzi himself did not want to serve in a royal capacity. He was a teacher, a thinker, a farmer, preferring the quiet life in ancient Haslam, a town founded hundreds of years ago at the base of the Tekti Mountains.

But when a neighboring country had sought to invade Saidia fifty some years ago, Sheikh Azizzi was one of the first to volunteer to defend his country and people. He'd spent nearly two years on the front line. Halfway through, he was wounded in battle, and yet he refused to leave his fellow soldiers, inspiring the dispirited Saidia troops to fight on.

After the war ended, Sheikh Azizzi returned home, refusing all gifts, and accolades, wanting no financial reward. He wasn't interested in being a popular figure. He didn't want attention, didn't feel he deserved the attention. What he wanted was truth, peace, and stability for all Saidia people.

"I will ask Sheikh Azizzi to be fair. I cannot ask for him to be compassionate," Mikael said suddenly, his voice deep and rough in the quiet of the car. "Compassion is too much like weakness. Compassion lacks muscle, and conviction."

"Does he know about my father, and what he did to your family?"

"Yes."

"So he won't be fair."

"Fair, according to our laws. Perhaps not fair according to yours."

For two hours the convoy of cars traveled across the wide stretch of desert, before turning southeast toward the foothills and then on to the Tekti mountain range. They traveled up a narrow winding road, through the steep mountain pass, before beginning their descent into the valley below.

Finally they were slowing, the cars leaving the main road for the walled town built at the foot of the mountains.

Jemma was very glad the cars were slowing. She needed fresh air. She needed water. She needed a chance to stretch her legs.

"Haslam," the sheikh announced.

She craned her head to get a better look at the town. Twenty-foot-tall walls surrounded it. Turrets and parapets peeked above the walls. The vehicles' headlights illuminated huge wooden gates. Slowly the massive gates opened and the convoy pulled into the village.

They drove a short way before the cars parked in front of a two-story building that looked almost identical to the buildings on either side.

Jemma frowned at the narrow house. It didn't look like a courthouse or official city building. It seemed very much like an ordinary home.

The driver came around the side of the car to open the back passenger door. "We will go in for tea and conversation, but no one here will speak English," Mikael said, adding bluntly, "and they won't understand you. Or your short skirt." He leaned from the car, spoke to the driver and the driver nodded, and disappeared.

"I'm getting you a robe," Mikael said turning back to her. "It won't help you to go before Sheikh Azizzi dressed like that. I am sure you know this already, but be quiet, polite. Respectful. You are the outsider here. You need to make a good impression."

"Sheikh Azizzi is here?"

"Yes."

"I'm meeting him *now*?"

"Yes."

Fresh panic washed through her. "I thought we were going in for tea and conversation!"

"We are. This is the judicial process. It's not in a court with many observers. It's more intimate…personal. We sit at a table, have tea, and talk. Sheikh Azizzi will either come to a decision during the discussion, or he will leave and make a decision and then return to tell us what he has chosen to do."

"And it really all rests with him?"

"Yes."

"Could you not override his decision? You are the king."

Mikael studied her impassively. "I could, but I doubt I would."

"Why?"

"He is a tribal judge, and the highest in my tribe. As Bedouin, we honor our tribal elders, and he is the most respected man from my tribe."

The driver returned with a dark blue folded cotton garment and handed it to Mikael. Mikael shook out the robe and told her to slip it over her head. "This is more conservative, and should make him feel more comfortable."

She reached up and touched her hair. "Shouldn't I have a headscarf too?"

"He knows you're American, knows your father was Daniel Copeland. No need to pretend to be someone you're not."

"But I also have no wish to further offend him."

"Then perhaps braid your hair and tie it with an elastic. But your hair is not going to protect you from judgment. Nothing will. This is fate. Karma."

Jemma swiftly braided her hair and then stepped from the car, following Mikael. *Fate. Karma.* The words rang through her head as she walked behind the sheikh toward the house.

Robed men and women lined the small dirt road, bowing

deeply. Mikael paused to greet them, speaking briefly and then waving to some children who peeked from windows upstairs before leading her to the arched door of the house. The door opened and they were ushered inside.

Candles and sconces on the wall illuminated the interior. The whitewashed walls were simple and unadorned. Dark beams covered the ceiling in the entry, but the beams had been painted cream and pale gold in the living room.

As Mikael and Jemma were taken to a low table in the living room, Jemma spotted more children peeking from behind a curtain before being drawn away.

"Sit here," Mikael instructed, pointing to a pillow on the floor in front of the low square table. "To my right. Sheikh Azizzi will sit across from me, and speak to me, but this way he can see you easily."

Jemma sank onto the pillow, curling her legs under her. "He's not going to ask me anything?"

"No. Over tea I will give him the facts. He will consider the facts and then make his decision."

"Is this how you handle all tribal crimes?"

"If it's not a violent crime, why should the sentencing be chaotic and violent?"

She smoothed the soft thin cotton fabric over her knees. "But your country has a long history of aggression. Tribal warring, kidnapped brides, forced marriages." She quickly glanced at him. "I'm not trying to be sarcastic. I ask the question sincerely. How does one balance your ideal of civility in sentencing, with what we Westerners would view as barbaric tribal customs?"

"You mean, kidnapped brides?"

Her eyes widened. "No. I was referring to arranged marriages."

He said nothing. She stared at him aghast. The seconds ticked by.

Jemma pressed her hands to her stomach, trying to calm the wild butterflies. "Do you really kidnap your brides?"

"If you are a member of one of the royal families, yes."

"You're serious?"

"Yes."

"*Why?*"

He shrugged. "It's how one protects the tribe, by forging new ties through forced marriage with other tribes."

"It's barbaric."

"It settles a score."

"You sound so cavalier about a very violent act."

"The marriage might be forced, but the sex is generally consensual." His dark gaze held hers. "One takes a bride to settle a debt, but the captive bride becomes a royal wife. The marriage must be satisfying for both."

"I sincerely doubt a forced marriage can ever be satisfying!"

"A forced marriage isn't that different from an arranged marriage, and that is also foreign to your Western way of thinking, so perhaps it's better if you do not judge."

A shadow filled the doorway and an older, robed man entered the living room.

Mikael rose, and hugged the older man. They clasped each other's arm and spoke in Arabic. After a moment both Mikael and Sheikh Azizzi sat down at the table, still deep in conversation.

Sheikh Azizzi hadn't even looked at her yet. Mikael didn't glance her way either.

Their conversation was grave. No laughter, no joking. They took turns speaking, first one, and then the other. The mood in the room was somber. Intense.

They were interrupted after fifteen minutes or so by a male servant carrying a tea tray. Sheikh Azizzi and Mikael ignored the man with the tray but Jemma was grateful to see the tea and biscuits and dried fruit arrive. She was hungry, and thirsty. She eyed the teacup placed in front of her and the plate of biscuits and fruit but didn't touch either one, waiting for a signal from Mikael, or Sheikh Azizzi. But neither glanced her way.

She longed for a sip but waited instead.

They talked for at least another fifteen minutes after the tea tray was brought in. The servant came back, carried away the now cold tea on the tray, and returned five minutes later with a fresh steaming pot.

Jemma's stomach growled. She wanted to nibble on one of the biscuits. She didn't even care what the tea tasted like. She just wanted a cup.

But she sat still, and practiced breathing as if she were in her yoga class in London. Instead of getting upset, she'd meditate.

Jemma closed her eyes, and focused on clearing her mind, and her breathing. She wouldn't think about anything, wouldn't worry...

"Drink your tea, Jemma," Mikael said abruptly.

She opened her eyes, looked at him, startled to hear him use her first name, and somewhat uneasy with his tone. It hadn't been a request. It'd been a command.

He expected her to obey.

Nervous, she reached for her tea, and sipped from the cup. The tea was lukewarm. It tasted bitter. But it wet her throat and she sipped the drink slowly, as the men continued talking.

Sheikh Azizzi was speaking now. His voice was deep and low. His delivery was measured, the pace of his words deliberate.

He's sentencing me, she thought, stomach cramping. *He's giving the judgment now.* She looked quickly at Mikael, trying to gauge his reaction.

But Mikael's expression was blank. He sipped his tea, and then again. After what felt like an endless silence, he answered. His answer wasn't very long. It didn't sound very complicated, but it did sound terse. He wasn't happy.

Jemma didn't know how she knew. She just knew.

Both men were silent. Sheikh Azizzi ate a dried apricot. They sipped more tea. There wasn't any conversation at this point.

Mikael placed his cup on the table and spoke at last. His voice was quiet, and even, but there was a firmness in his tone that hadn't been there earlier. Sheikh Azizzi replied to Mikael. A very short reply.

A small muscle pulled in Mikael Karim's jaw. His lips thinned. He spoke. It sound like a one syllable reply. A fierce one syllable reply.

She glanced from Azizzi to Mikael and back. The two men stared at each other, neither face revealing any expression. After a moment, Sheikh Azizzi murmured something and rose, exiting the room and leaving Mikael and Jemma alone.

CHAPTER FOUR

THAT DID NOT go well.

Aware that Jemma was looking at him, aware that she'd been waiting patiently, exceptionally patiently for the past hour to know her fate, Mikael finally glanced at her.

Shadows danced on the walls, stretching tall across the tiled floor. He didn't like her. Didn't admire her. Didn't feel anything positive for her.

But even in the dim lighting, he recognized her great beauty.

She wasn't merely pretty, she was stunning. Her face was all hauntingly beautiful planes and angles with her high regal brow, the prominent cheekbones, a firm chin below full, generous lips.

She was pale with fatigue and fear, and her pallor made her eyes appear even greener, as if brilliant emeralds against the ivory satin of her skin.

Sitting so close to her, he could feel her fatigue. It was clear to him she was stretched thin, perhaps even to breaking.

He told himself he didn't care, but her beauty moved him. His mother had been a beautiful woman, too, just as Mikael's father's second and third wives were both exquisite. A king could have any woman. Why shouldn't she be a rare jewel?

Jemma was a rare jewel.

But she was also a rare jewel set in a tarnished, defective setting.

He now had a choice. To save the jewel, or to toss it away? It was up to him. Sheikh Azizzi had given Mikael the decision.

"Well?" Jemma whispered, breaking the tense silence. "What did he say?"

Mikael continued to study her, his thoughts random and scattered. He didn't need her. He didn't like her. He'd never love her.

But he did desire her.

It wouldn't be difficult to bed her.

He wondered how she'd respond in bed. He wondered if she'd be sweet and hot or icy and frigid.

His gut told him she'd be hot and sweet. But first, all the Copeland taint would have to be washed away. "I am to decide your punishment for you," he said finally. "I've been given a choice of two sentences and I must pick one."

"Why?"

"Because Sheikh Azizzi knows me, and he knows I wish to do what is right, but what is right isn't always what is popular."

"I don't understand."

"I am to decide if I should follow ancient law, and tribal custom, or choose a modern punishment for you."

"And have you made up your mind?"

"No."

"What are the choices given to you?"

"Seven years house arrest here in Haslam—"

"*Seven* years?"

"Or I take you as my wife."

"That's not funny. Not even remotely funny."

"It's not a joke. It's one of the two choices presented to me. Marry you, or leave you here in Haslam to begin your house arrest." He saw her recoil and her face turn white. "I warned you that Sheikh Azizzi would not be lenient. He is not a Copeland fan either. He knows what your father did to my mother, and he wanted to send a message that Saidia will not tolerate crime or immorality."

"But seven years!" She reached for the edge of the table to steady herself. "That's...that's...so long."

"Seven years, *or* marriage," he corrected.

"No. No. Marriage isn't an option. I won't marry you. I would never marry you. I could never marry you—"

"You'd rather be locked up for seven years?"

"*Yes.* Absolutely!"

Mikael leaned back, studying her pale face and bright eyes. She was biting down, pressing her teeth into her lip. "I don't believe you."

"Not my problem."

"I'm a king. I can provide a lavish lifestyle."

"Not interested." Her eyes burned at him, hot, bright. "Seven years of house arrest is infinitely better than a lifetime with you."

He should have been offended by her response. Instead he felt vaguely amused. Women craved his attention. They fought for his affections. Ever since he'd left university, he'd enjoyed considerable female company, company he'd turned into girlfriends and mistresses.

Mikael enjoyed women. He was quite comfortable with girlfriends and mistresses. But he was not at all open to taking a wife, despite the fact that as king it was his duty to marry and produce heirs.

Something he was sure Sheikh Azizzi knew. But Sheikh Azizzi, like much of Saidia, was eager for the country's king to marry as quickly as possible.

Sheikh Azizzi also knew that nothing would pain the Copeland family more than having the youngest daughter forced into a marriage against her will.

It was fitting punishment for a family that believed itself to be above the law.

But in truth Mikael didn't want a wife. He didn't want children. He didn't want entanglements of any kind. It's why he kept mistresses. He provided for them materially and in return they'd always be available to him, without making any demands. Mikael was torn between his duty and his desires.

He studied Jemma now, trying to imagine *her* as his wife.

Without her make-up he could see purple smudges beneath

her eyes and her naturally long black eye lashes. She had a heart-shaped face. Clear green eyes. Full pink lips.

The same pink as her nipples.

His body hardened, remembering her earlier, modeling, and naked beneath the fur coat.

She had an incredible body.

He would enjoy her body. But he'd never like her. Never admire her. She wasn't a woman he wanted for anything beyond sex and pleasure.

He pictured her naked again. He'd certainly find pleasure in her curves and breasts and that private place between her legs.

"So it's house arrest," Jemma said. "Seven years. Would the sentence start tonight? Tomorrow?"

"I haven't made up my mind," he answered.

Her green eyes widened. Her lips parted and for a moment no sound came out and then she shook her head, a frantic shake that left no doubt as to her feelings. "I will not marry you. I will not!"

"It's not up to you. It's my choice."

"You can't force me."

"I can." And silently he added, *I could*.

Just like that, the idea took root.

He could marry her. He could force her to his will. He could avenge his mother's shame. He could exact revenge.

For a moment there was just silence. It was thick and heavy and he imagined she must hate it. She must find the silence stifling because she was completely powerless. She had no say. He would decide her fate. She would have to accept whatever he chose for her.

He found the thought pleasing.

He liked knowing that whatever he chose, she would have to submit.

She with the lovely eyes and soft lips and full, pink tipped breasts.

"But you do not wish to marry me," she whispered. "You hate me. You wouldn't be able to look at me or touch me."

"I could touch you," he corrected. "And I could look at you. But I wouldn't love you, no."

"Don't do that to me. Don't use me."

"Why not? Your father used my mother to bring shame on my family name."

"I'm not my father and you're not your mother and we both deserve better. We both deserve good marriages, proper marriages, marriages based on love and respect."

"That sounds quite nice except for the fact that I don't love. I won't take a wife out of love. I will take her out of duty. I will marry as it is my responsibility. A king must have heirs."

"But I want love. And by forcing me to marry you, you deprive me of love."

"Your father deprived my mother of life. I'm Arabic. A life for a life. A woman for a woman. He took her. I *should* take you."

"No."

"Saidia requires a prince. You'd give me beautiful children."

"I'd never be willing in bed, and you said even in a forced marriage, the sex is consensual."

"You'd consent."

"I wouldn't."

"You'd beg me to take you."

"Never."

The corner of his mouth lifted. "You're wrong. And I will prove you wrong, and when I do, what shall you give me in return?"

Jemma rose from the table, and went to the doorway. "I want to go. I want to go now."

"I don't think that's one of my options."

Jemma didn't know where to look. Her heart raced and her eyes burned and she felt so sick inside.

This wasn't what she'd thought would happen. This wasn't how she'd imagined this would go. Jail was bad. Seven years under house arrest boggled the mind. But *marriage*?

The idea of Sheikh Karim forcing her to marry him made everything inside her shrink, collapse.

She'd thought the last year had been horrific, being shunned as Daniel Copeland's daughter, but to be married against her will?

Her eyes stung, growing hotter and grittier. She pressed her nails into her palms, determined not to cry, even as she wondered how far she'd get if she bolted from the house and ran.

Marrying Mikael Karim would break her. It would. She'd been so lonely this past year, so deeply hurt by Damien's rejection and the constant shaming by the media, as well as endless public hatred. She couldn't face a cold marriage. She needed to live, to move, to breathe, to feel, to love...

To love.

It was tragic but she needed love. Needed to love and be loved. Needed connection and contact and warmth.

"Please," she choked, the tears she didn't want filling her eyes, "please don't marry me. Please just leave me here in Haslam. I don't want to spend seven years here, but at least in seven years I could be free and go home and marry and have children with someone who wants me, and needs me, and loves me—" She broke off as Sheikh Azizzi entered the room behind her.

The village elder was accompanied by two robed men.

Jemma pressed her hands together in prayer, pleading with Mikael. "Let me stay here. Please. *Please.*"

"And what would you do here for seven years?" he retorted, ignoring the others.

"I'd learn the language, and learn to cook and I'd find ways to occupy myself."

Mikael looked at her, his dark gaze holding for an endless moment and then he turned to Sheikh Azizzi and spoke to him. Sheikh Azizzi nodded once and the men walked out.

"It's done," Mikael said.

"What's done?"

"I've claimed you. I've made you mine."

She backed up so rapidly she bumped into the wall. *"No."*

"But I have. I told Sheikh Azizzi I've claimed you as my wife, and it's done."

"That doesn't make us married. I have to agree, I have to speak, I have to consent somehow..." Her voice trailed off. She stared at Mikael, bewildered. "Don't I?"

"No. You don't have to speak at all. It's done."

"Just like that?"

"Just like that." He rose and stalked toward her. "And like this," he added, sweeping her into his arms and carrying her out of the house, into the night.

Outside, the convoy of vehicles were gone. Villagers clustered near a kneeling camel.

"Who is that for?" Jemma choked, struggling in Mikael's arms.

He tightened his grip. "Settle down," he said shortly. "Or I'll tie you to the camel."

"You wouldn't!"

"You don't think so?" he challenged, stepping through the crowd to set her in the camel's saddle.

The leather saddle was wide and hard and Jemma struggled to climb back off but Mikael had taken a leather strip from a pouch on the camel and was swiftly tying her hands together at the wrist, and then binding her wrists to the saddle's pommel.

The crowd cheered as he tethered her in place.

"Why are they cheering?" she asked, face burning, anger rolling through her as she strained to free herself.

"They know I've taken you as my wife. They know you aren't happy. They know you are ashamed. It pleases them."

"My shame pleases them?"

"Your shame and struggles are part of your atonement. *That* pleases them."

"I don't like your culture."

"And I do not like yours." He scooted her forward in the saddle, and then took a seat behind her, his big body filling the space, pressing tightly against her. "Now lean back a little."

"No."

"You'll be more comfortable."

"I can assure you, I would not be comfortable leaning against you."

"We are going to be traveling for several hours."

She shook her head, lips compressed as she fought tears. "I hate you," she whispered.

"I wouldn't have it any other way." He gave a tug on the reigns and the camel lurched to its feet.

The villagers cheered again and Mikael lifted a hand, and then they were off, heading for the gates and the desert beyond.

CHAPTER FIVE

THEY RODE FOR what felt like hours through an immense desert of undulating dunes beneath a three quarter moon. The moon's bright light illuminated the desert, painting the dunes a ghostly white.

Jemma tried to hold herself stiff and straight to avoid touching Sheikh Karim but it was impossible as time wore on, just as it was impossible to ignore his warmth stealing into her body.

A half hour into the journey she broke the silence. "Where are we going?"

"My Kasbah. My home," he said. "One of my homes," he corrected.

"Why this one?"

"It is where all Karims spend their honeymoon."

She didn't know what to say to that. She didn't know what to think, or feel. So much had happened in the past few hours that she felt numb and overwhelmed.

Part of her brain whispered she was in trouble, and yet another part hadn't accepted any of this.

It didn't make sense, this forced marriage. She kept thinking any moment she'd wake up and discover it a strange dream.

Her captor was big and solid, his chest muscular, his arms strong, biceps taut as he held her steady in the saddle, his broad back protecting her from the cold.

He struck her as powerful but not brutal. Fierce and yet not insensitive.

In a different situation she might even like him. In a different situation she might like the spicy exotic fragrance he wore. In a different situation she might find him darkly beautiful.

But it wasn't a different situation. There was no way she could find him attractive, or appealing. She wasn't attracted to him, or the hard planes of his chest, or even aware of the way his muscular thighs cradled her, pinning her between his hips and the saddle's pommel.

They lapsed back into a silence neither tried to break. But an hour later, Mikael, shifted, drawing her closer to him. "There," he said. "My home."

Jemma stared hard into the dark, but could see nothing. "Where?"

"Straight in front of us."

But there was nothing in front of them. Just sand. "I don't see—"

"Watch."

The brilliant moonlight rippled across the desert, bathing all in ghostly white.

And then little by little the desert revealed a long wall, and then a bit later she was able to see shapes behind the wall. The shapes became shadowy clay buildings.

In the middle of the night, in the glow of moonlight, it looked like a lost world. As if they'd traveled back in time.

She sucked in a nervous breath as they approached massive wooden gates cut into the towering clay walls. Two enormous gas lanterns hung on either side of the dark wooden gate, and Mikael shouted out in Arabic as they reached them, and just like that, the gates split, and slowly opened, revealing square turrets and towers within.

Robed people poured into the courtyard as the gates were shut and locked behind them.

They were lining up before the first building with its immense keyhole doorway, bowing repeatedly.

"What's happening?" she whispered.

"We're being welcomed by my people. They have heard I've brought home my bride."

The camel stopped moving. Robed men moved forward. Mikael threw the reins and one of the men took it, and commanded the camel to kneel.

Sheikh Karim jumped off the camel, and then turned to look at her. His gaze held hers, his expression fierce. "What we have just done is life changing. But we've made a commitment, and we shall honor that commitment."

Then he swung her into his arms and carried her through the tall door of his Kasbah, into a soaring entrance hall, its high white plaster ceiling inset with blue and gold mosaic tile.

He set her on her feet, and added, "Welcome, my wife, to your new home."

A slender robed female servant led Jemma through the Kasbah's labyrinth of empty halls. The maid was silent. Jemma was grateful for the silence, exhausted from the long day and hours of travel. The last time she'd glanced at her watch it had been just after midnight, and that had to be at least an hour ago now.

The silent maid led Jemma down one hallway to another, until they reached a white high ceilinged room with walls covered in delicate ivory latticework. The bed's silk coverlet was also white and stitched with threads of the palest gold and silver, while silver and white silk curtains hung on either side of the tall French doors which opened to a courtyard of ivory stone and planters filled with palms, gardenias and white hibiscus.

The room wasn't huge but it was opulent, elegant, and blissfully serene, an inviting, soothing oasis after a grueling and frightening day.

"Tea? Refreshment, Your Highness?" the maid asked in polite, accented English.

Your Highness?

Jemma glanced behind her, expecting Mikael to be there. But no one stood behind Jemma. The room was empty.

And then it hit her. The maid was speaking to her. They

all knew she'd married Mikael, then. They all knew she was
his bride…

Would he come to her tonight? Did he expect to consum-
mate the marriage tonight?

Jemma sank down on one of the white sofas in the sitting
area, no longer sure her legs would support her.

"No, thank you," she said. "I'm fine. I think I just want to
sleep."

"Shall I draw you a bath before I leave?"

Still dazed, Jemma nodded. "Yes, please."

A few minutes later the maid had gone and steam wafted
from the bathroom, fragrant with lilacs and verbena.

Jemma entered the grand white marble and tiled bathroom
with the gleaming gold fixtures, the sunken tub illuminated
by a multitude of dazzling crystal chandeliers above.

Awed by the grandeur, she stripped off her dusty robe and
gritty clothes and slid into the water for a soak.

The hot scented bath felt so good after the jarring camel
ride that Jemma was reluctant to leave the bath until the water
began to cool. By the time she finally pulled the plug, she could
barely keep her eyes open another moment.

Wrapped in an enormous plush white towel she returned to
her bedroom, not at all sure what she'd wear to sleep in, and
there on the oversized bed was a simple white cotton nightgown with lace trim at the shoulders and hem.

Jemma slipped the nightgown over her head, gave her long
hair another quick towel-dry and then climbed beneath the soft
smooth cotton coverlet, desperate to sleep. She didn't even remember trying to fall asleep. She was out within minutes of
turning off her bedside lamp.

She was still sleeping deeply when woken by a firm, insistent knock on the outer door.

Opening her eyes, she frowned at the dimly lit room, confused by what she saw. It took her a moment to figure out
where she was. Sheikh Karim's Kasbah.

And then she remembered—she'd married him.

Or so he'd said. She didn't feel married. She didn't feel anything at all but sleepy and numb.

Jemma slid her legs from the bed and slipped on the white robe she'd seen draped over a chair before she answered the outer door.

It was Mikael.

"Good afternoon," he said.

She tucked a tangled strand of hair behind her ear. "Afternoon?"

"It's after two."

"Is it? I can't believe it."

"I've ordered coffee to be sent to you, and then you're to join me for a late lunch in the east pavilion. Don't be late." He turned and walked toward the door, but Jemma followed.

"That sounds rather rude, Sheikh Karim," she said, following after him. "Is that how you speak to all your women?"

He glanced at her. "I'm accustomed to being in charge."

"That's fine, but you don't need to be quite so aggressive. A little kindness and courtesy can go a long way."

"I thought I was being kind and courteous by sending coffee to you."

"Yes, but then you ruined it by ordering me to join you, tacking on a warning not to be late. It would have been much nicer if you'd simply asked me to join you in thirty minutes."

"Kings do not ask, Jemma. They command."

"I'm sorry, but I didn't marry a king. I married a man. That is, if we are truly married…"

"We are married. Quite married. As married as one can be in Saidia," he said, cutting her off, and walking back toward her. "But if it takes our consummating the marriage to feel married, then so be it. Tonight I will take you to my bed and there won't be any question in your mind afterwards."

"That's not what I want!"

"How do you know? You've never been in my bed. I think once you are there, you'll like it very much." And then he was gone.

* * *

The next half hour seemed endless to Jemma. He was planning on consummating the marriage tonight?

But she didn't even know him.

She couldn't imagine having sex with him.

He couldn't be serious.

And yet here she was, in the Kasbah, being waited on hand and foot, so she didn't doubt him anymore. He wasn't a man who made jokes. He meant what he said, which meant…

He intended to bed her tonight.

Jemma's clothes from last night had been washed and dried and returned to her. She dressed in the short skirt and blouse, and then slipped her feet into her high wedges. Her hair was wild, a thick tangle of waves from falling asleep with it still wet, and she subdued the waves as best as she could, pulling the long mass into a ponytail and then adding some fat silver bangles to her wrist and simple silver hoops to her ears. Not very fancy but it was the best she could do.

And then the maid knocked on the door. She'd returned to escort Jemma to lunch, leading her through the maze of hallways and halls to a door that led outside to a beautiful walled garden shaded by palms with a tiled fountain in the center of the courtyard.

Mikael was already there, waiting for her.

"I recognize those clothes," he said.

"It's all I have with me."

"I had some gowns put in your wardrobe."

"I didn't see them," she answered, aware that she hadn't looked, either.

He was silent a moment, studying her. "We need to talk, but you also need to eat, so we shall sit, and eat, and talk and hopefully become better acquainted so this wedding night will be more…comfortable…for you."

She made a soft sound of protest. "I don't think eating and talking will make anything about tonight comfortable. I can't believe this is real. Can't believe any of this is happening. I didn't say any vows. I didn't agree to anything."

"You didn't have to. I claimed you and that was all that was needed. My word is law."

"That makes for a very quick and convenient ceremony."

"The ceremony might be quick, but the honeymoon isn't. We will stay together here for sixteen days before we return to my palace in the capitol."

"You don't even like me. How can you contemplate bedding me?"

His lips quirked. It was as close to a smile as she had ever seen from him. "You are not an unattractive woman, Jemma. And I'm sure you are quite aware that a man can desire a woman without engaging one's emotions."

"So when you bed me tonight, it will be without tenderness or passion."

"If you are worried about the act itself, you needn't be. I am a skillful lover. I will take my time and be sure to satisfy your needs. It wouldn't be a proper honeymoon if I didn't."

A proper honeymoon.

A proper honeymoon was the trip to Bali with Damien. They'd already booked their air and hotels when he'd broken it off. She'd planned a wedding that hadn't taken place. And now she was married without a wedding and trapped here for a honeymoon she didn't want.

Her eyes burned. Her throat ached. Jemma blinked and looked away, across the courtyard, to the splashing fountain. The water danced and trickled and it amazed her that the water could be so light and tinkling when her heart felt so heavy and broken.

"I don't want to be pleasured," she whispered, reaching up to brush away a tear before it could fall. "I don't want any of this."

"You will become less resistant to the idea as time goes on."

She choked on a hysterical laugh as she glanced at him. "You think?"

He shrugged. "I imagine for you, being from a Western culture, this is terribly strange, but it is not as strange for me. I hadn't ever expected to marry for love. I've known all along that my bride would be from a different tribe. I just didn't expect it to be...yours."

"The despised Copelands."

"Fortunately, you are no longer a Copeland, but a Karim. You've left your family and are now a member of mine. You have a new name. A new start. And new responsibilities. I think it will be good for you." He gestured to the table in the shade. "We can talk more, as we eat. Sit—" he broke off, even as her eyebrows arched.

His lips curved grimly. He gave her a slight bow. "Forgive me," he drawled, not sounding the least bit apologetic. "Let *us* sit. We should try to be comfortable."

She didn't like his tone, and she hated the situation. Nothing about this was right. She would have gladly picked jail or house arrest over being trapped with him. "I can't eat. I'm too upset."

"Then I shall eat, and you can watch, because I am hungry."

"And you wonder why I'm not excited about this honeymoon."

"Yes, I do wonder. By choosing you as my first wife, I've made you a queen. You are wealthy beyond measure. That should please you to no end."

"I've had money. I don't care about money. I care about kindness, and decency. Strength. Compassion. Integrity."

"I have all that, too, so you're in luck. Now, let's eat."

"You are not compassionate."

"I am, for those requiring compassion. But you, my queen, do not need my compassion. You are doing an excellent job feeling sorry for yourself already."

She exhaled in a quick rush. "You lack sensitivity, Sheikh Karim."

"Possibly, as well as patience. Particularly when I am hungry." His dark gaze met hers and held. "But you are only making this more difficult for yourself. Fighting me, fighting the marriage, fighting to accept that we are married and that this marriage is real. I take our vows very seriously."

"What vows? I said none!"

"I claimed you, I've married you," he said, "and so it is done. Now sit. Before I carry you to the table myself."

Reluctantly, unwillingly, Jemma took a seat at the low table inside the shaded pavilion kept cool by overhead fans.

She hadn't thought she could eat, but the first course of chilled soup settled her stomach and she was able to eat some of the grilled meat and vegetables in the second and third courses. She felt better with food, calmer and less jittery. But even then, she was in shock. She thought she'd be in shock for quite some time.

There wasn't much conversation during the meal, which was fine with her. Instead Mikael studied her from across the table as if he were a scientist and she an animal he was observing.

He was the animal, though.

Maybe not an animal. But he was the one that was untamed and unpredictable. The very air around him seemed to snap and crackle with energy and tension, making the soft afternoon light dangerous, mysterious, while her heart raced and her pulse drummed, too thick and quick in her veins.

"Saidia is nothing like your country. Saidia is still essentially tribal in culture," Mikael said, as the last of the dishes were cleared away and he rinsed his fingers in a bowl of hot scented water and dried them on a soft cloth before sending the bowl and towel away. "I expect it will take you time to adjust to our culture, but you must keep an open mind. Our customs will be foreign to you but there is a reason for everything, and value to everything we do."

"And that includes kidnapping one's bride?"

"Most definitely."

"I don't see how kidnapping a woman can ever be justified. Women are not objects, not property."

"Only princes and kings, members of the royal family, kidnap a young woman for marriage."

"That's even worse."

He shook his head. "The custom of kidnapping one's bride goes back a thousand years. It helps protect one's family and society by strengthening tribal relations, forging bonds between rival tribes, protecting one's women and children from nomad tribes that might seek to prey on vulnerable tribes."

"I'm sorry. I still can't wrap my head around the custom."

"Many of Saidia's young people joke about the ancient customs when attending university, but if you asked them if forced marriages and arranged marriages should be banned, not one of them would vote to have them outlawed. It's part of our history. It's a big part of our cultural identity."

"So not all Saidia citizens have an arranged marriage?"

"About half of our young people in the urban areas choose a love marriage. If you move away from the big cities, nearly everyone prefers arranged marriages."

"Why the difference?"

He shrugged. "In the desert, people strongly identify with their tribe and tribal customs. You don't have the influence of technology. Towns are remote. Travel is difficult and change is viewed with suspicion. When you come to Haslam or the other desert communities south of the Takti Mountains, it's like traveling back in time. Haslam isn't the city capitol. The desert isn't urban. And I, as the king, must be sensitive to the new and old faces of my country. I can't alienate the youth in the city, but I must also respect the youth in the desert."

"They don't both want the same thing?"

"They don't want the same thing, nor do they understand each other. It's been a struggle for us, in terms of keeping Saidia connected. When our students are ten, we try to encourage the children to do an exchange; children from the desert leaving home to spend a week in the city with a host family, and the children in the city to go to the desert for a week. It used to be mandated but that became problematic. We still want children to participate, but our city children are bored by the desert and the lack of entertainment, and the children from the desert are overwhelmed by the city noise, pollution, and frenetic activity."

"So what do you do?"

"Try to respect both aspects of the Saidia culture, and be careful not to alienate either."

"It's a balancing act," she said.

"Absolutely." He studied her a long moment, his gaze slowly sweeping from her face down to her shoulders and then breasts. "I don't want to see you in those clothes anymore. I have provided you with a wardrobe, a more suitable wardrobe for the climate, the Kasbah, and our honeymoon."

Jemma had just begun to relax, forgetting her own situation having been pleasantly distracted by the discussion, but suddenly reality came crashing back. She tensed, flushed, angered as well as frustrated. "Is that a request or a command, Your Highness?"

"Both."

"It can't be both. It's either one or the other."

He gave his dark head a shake. "There you go again, making it difficult. You don't need to resist so much."

"Oh, I do. I most certainly do. I'm not a doll, or a mindless puppet. I'm an adult, a woman, and very independent. I've been on my own, and paying my own bills, since I was eighteen. I value my independence, too."

"I appreciate spirit, but there is a difference between spark, stubbornness and plain stupidity." He lifted his hand to stop her before she could speak. "And no, I'm not saying you are stupid. But right now you're stubborn. If the stubbornness continues too much longer, then yes, you've moved into stupidity."

Her cheeks burned. Her temper blazed. "I could say the same for you. You are equally stubborn in your refusal to see me for who I am."

"I see exactly who you are."

"A criminal Copeland!"

"No." He leaned forward, his dark gaze boring into her. "My wife."

Something in his words and fierce, intense gaze stripped her of speech and the ability to think.

For a moment she simply sat there, dazed, and breathless.

"You *are* going to experience culture shock," he said firmly, "but I fully expect you to adjust. We will be here until you adjust. So instead of arguing with me about everything, I think it is time you tried to be more open minded about this, us, and marriage to a Saidia king."

"I'm trying."

"No, I don't think you are, not yet. But I have all day. We have all day. We have all night. We have weeks, actually."

Her lips pressed firm. She glanced away, studying the exotic pink and blue mosaic tile work on the inside of the pavilion. The tiles were beautiful, the colors gorgeous, and unabashedly romantic. The remote Kasbah would have been extremely romantic if she were here, with someone else. Someone like Damien.

She still loved him.

Or maybe, she still loved who she thought he had been. Loving, strong, protective.

Turned out he wasn't so loving. Or protective. His strength was an illusion…all beautiful body and muscle but no core. No spine. No backbone, at least not when it was needed.

"You're not going to cry, are you?" Mikael asked, a hint of roughness in his deep voice.

She shook her head hard. "No."

"You're looking very sad at the moment. Thoroughly crushed. Don't tell me that twelve hours of marriage to me has broken you already."

Jemma jerked her chin up. "Not crushed, or broken. Nor will I be. I won't give any man that kind of power over me."

"Not even that pretty model ex-boyfriend of yours?"

Jemma stifled a gasp. So Mikael had done his research then, and discovered her humiliation at the hands of Damien. She lifted her chin defiantly.

"Especially not him." ·

"Mmm." But Mikael didn't sound as if he believed her.

"Damien hurt me, but he didn't break me. And my father hurt me, but he didn't break me. And you, Sheikh Karim, might intimidate me, and bully me, but you will not break me, either."

"I do not bully you."

"Oh yes, you do. At least, you try to."

He leaned farther back into the pillows surrounding the low table. The corner of his mouth curved. "You really aren't afraid of me?"

"Why should I be afraid? You're Drakon's friend. You came to his wedding. You saved me from seven years of jail."

He must have heard the ironic note in her voice because the corners of his mouth quirked, and that faint lift of his lips made her heart suddenly do a strange double thump.

The man was extremely intimidating, and yet when he smiled, even this faint half-smile, he became dangerously attractive.

"Ah, yes, I saved you from jail. And you, my queen, are so very grateful."

She didn't miss his sarcasm. "I would have been more grateful if you'd put me on a plane back to London. That would have been nice."

"Indeed, it would have been. But terribly weak on my part. A man must have morals, and principles, and a king even more so."

She stood up and paced restlessly around the pavilion. She knew he watched her. She glanced at him and saw the same, faint smile playing at his lips, eyes gleaming. He seemed amused or entertained. Maybe both. "You're in a good mood," she said, facing him from across the pavilion.

"Would you prefer it if I were in a bad mood?"

Jemma didn't need to think about that one too much. "No, but surely you didn't anticipate taking a Copeland daughter for your wife?"

"That is correct. But you are easy to look at, and I am quite certain, a pleasure to hold."

"That sounds terribly shallow."

His broad shoulders shifted. "It's not a love match. I don't have to like you, or love you. I just need you, as my first wife, to be good, obedient and fertile."

She stiffened and looked at him askance. *First wife*? There would be others? "Multiple wives, Your Highness?"

"Traditional Islamic law allows men four wives, but a man must be able to treat them equally. And not all men choose to have multiple wives. It's really an individual decision."

She couldn't help laughing. It struck her as terribly wrong, and yet also, terribly funny. This wasn't her life. This couldn't be happening. He might as well have plucked her from the photo shoot and locked her in his harem. "Do you intend to take more wives?"

"I haven't thought that far, but my father had four wives. My grandfather, his father, just had two."

But two wives was still one too many.

She shot him a swift glance, trying to decide if he was joking. She hoped he was. Or hoped he'd come to his senses and let her return home. "I thought the practice of polygamy had been outlawed in modern Arab countries," she said, leaning against one of the columns supporting the pavilion arches.

"Tunisia did, yes," he agreed, "But most other countries have focused on reform. In Iraq, a man can take a second wife if he obtains permission from the government, while Morocco and Lebanon have added a clause in the premarital contract, allowing a woman to divorce her husband if he takes a second wife without her consent."

"Were your father's wives happy?"

He reached for a bite of mango from the platter of dried and fresh fruit. "Most of them. He was an excellent provider. But my father was also good to them. Respectful. Tried to please them. Refused to beat them."

Jemma's jaw dropped. "And that constitutes a good husband?"

His dark eyes met hers across the table. He arched a brow. "Don't you think so?"

"No."

"Marriage in Saidia is a duty. It's our duty to have children. It is through marriage we gain family, and family is our most cherished institution. Family is everything here. You protect your family at all costs." He paused for a half second. "Which is how your father failed you. He refused to protect you."

CHAPTER SIX

MIKAEL STUDIED JEMMA as she leaned against the column, her face turned away from him, giving him just her profile.

The late afternoon sun dappled her with light and shadows. He was too far away to see the freckles across the bridge of her nose but he imagined them there, as well as the soft pink of her lips.

Looking at her from across the pavilion made him remember her working yesterday, posing for that Australian photographer. She'd been so fierce and determined as the sun beat down on her, baking her inside the fur and thigh-high boots. But she hadn't complained, nor had she as they'd traveled by camel to the Kasbah late last night, her slim warm body against his chest and thighs. He'd felt protective of her last night as they'd crossed the desert. He'd been aware of the dangers in the desert, but even more aware of her.

Last night she'd stirred now and then, restless, and probably uncomfortable, but she hadn't uttered a word. He'd respected her for that.

He had wished she wouldn't wiggle though, as each time she shifted in his arms, her back had rubbed against his chest, and her small, firm backside had pressed against his groin.

He had tried not to think about her firm backside, her rounded hips or her full soft breasts, which he'd seen in all their glory earlier.

And now she was his wife. His bride.

The villagers of Haslam had been happy for him. His people wanted him settled. They wanted him to have children. They wanted to know that there was an heir, and a spare, and then another dozen more. They were also glad he'd taken a bride, following tradition. Tradition was still so very important in Saidia.

Mikael's gaze followed the play of sunlight and shadows over her body. She looked lithe and lovely in her clothes. He was looking forward to getting her out of them. He wondered what she'd be like in bed.

"Do you really hate him?" he asked, reaching for a date and rolling it between his fingers.

"My father?" she asked, clarifying his question.

"Yes."

Her shoulders twisted and she looked away, turning her head so that he could see just the curve of her ear and the line of her smooth jaw. "He did terrible things," she whispered.

Mikael said nothing.

Jemma drew a deep breath, her chest aching, her heart blistered. "But no, I don't hate him. I hate what he did to us. I hate what he did to those who trusted him. But he's my father, the only father I've ever known, and years ago, when I was little, he was like a king. Handsome, and charming and powerful, but also fun. For my fifth birthday, he brought the circus to me. We had a whole circus set up in our front yard with a big top tent, and acrobats and clowns and everything. He organized that. He made it happen." She sighed. "My parents divorced just before I turned six. I didn't see him very much after that."

"So he was a good father when you were little?"

"In a young child's eyes, yes. But during the divorce the battle lines were drawn and I, due to my age, went to Mother. All of us went with Mother, except Morgan, who chose to live with our father."

"Do you know why your parents divorced?"

Jemma hesitated. "I think he wasn't faithful."

"Was the divorce quite bitter?"

"Not as acrimonious as it could have been. They divided up kids and property and went on with their lives."

"But neither married again."

"No. Mother was too upset—she'd loved my father—and he didn't want to lose any more assets."

"This is why love marriages are dangerous. Far better to go in with a contract and no romantic illusions, than enter the marriage with impossible hopes and dreams of a fairy tale relationship that can't exist."

"But in an arranged marriage there is no love."

"Love isn't necessary for a good marriage. In fact, love would just make things more difficult."

"How shall I fulfill…my duties…without love?"

For a moment he was baffled, and then amused. Her point of view was so peculiarly Western. As if only those who had a romantic relationship could find satisfaction in bed. "Love isn't necessary for physical pleasure."

Jemma saw him rise from the cushions and walk around the table. She swallowed hard as he approached her, not knowing where to look, or what to do. Her heart was pounding and her brain felt scrambled.

"Marriage isn't all bad," he added quietly, circling her. "Our marriage will honor you. You are my queen. The first lady in my land. There will be no more public scorn. No more shaming. You will be protected."

His voice was a deep, low rumble, the pitch husky and strangely seductive. Jemma turned her head, watched his mouth. His firm lips suddenly fascinated her. "Until you take your next wife," she said, feeling almost breathless.

"Would you feel differently if you were my only wife?" he asked, reaching out to lift a dark strand of hair from her eyelashes and tuck it carefully behind her ear, his fingertips then caressing the curve of her ear before falling away.

His skin had been so warm, and his touch had been light,

fleeting, and yet she'd felt it all the way through her, a ripple of pleasure.

Aware that she'd never survive, not if she remained this close, Jemma moved away, crossing to the far end of the pavilion where the light was even more dappled. "Are you saying I would be your only wife?" she asked.

"I never planned on taking more than one wife," he answered.

"If you hoped to reassure me, you're not succeeding."

"Do you need reassurance? Is that what this is about?" He was moving toward her again, walking slowly, confidently, relaxed and yet still somehow regal.

Jemma's heart hammered harder as he closed the distance. She didn't feel safe. She didn't feel comfortable or in control.

He didn't stop walking until he was directly in front of her, less than a foot away. "There is always anxiety on a honeymoon," he added, his voice dropping, his tone soothing. "It is natural to feel fear…even reluctance. But you will soon realize there is nothing to be afraid of. You will discover you can trust me. That you are safe with me. Safe to explore your fantasies."

"No!" Her voice spiked as she put a hand out to stop him, unable to imagine exploring any fantasies with him. This was so overwhelming. "This is too much, moving too fast."

She pushed past him to leave the pavilion and step into the sun. She felt his gaze follow her. "You need to give me time," she insisted. "You need to let me come to terms with everything."

"You've had the day."

She spun around. "No, it's not even been a full day. I was asleep until just a couple hours ago. You're not being fair. I need time. Time to accept the changes. Time to accept this new future."

"You will have that time, but you do not need to spend it alone. I think it is essential we spend time together, forming a relationship, and creating the foundation for our future."

She made a soft sound of protest. "How do you expect us

to have a relationship when there is no give or take? When you make the demands and insist on compliance? How can we have anything when you have all the power and control?"

"My power will never be used to hurt you. My power protects you, just as it protected you on the shoot, and then again in Haslam."

"You say you will protect me, but you forget what I'm sacrificing...my independence, my career, my friends, my hopes, my dreams." She shook her head. "But how do I know you will truly protect me? How do I know I can trust you when you use your power to subjugate my will?"

He looked at her, eyebrows lifted. "Because I've given you my word. My word is law."

"In Saidia, maybe. But I'm not Arab or Bedouin. I'm American. And my father said many things, but as we both know, he meant none of them. Damien said more things, promising me love and safety and security, and he didn't mean them, either. So no, I don't trust you. But that's because I don't trust men. How can I? Why should you be any different?"

He didn't speak, but this time he was listening. Carefully. Closely.

"You want a good wife," she said breathlessly. "Well, I want a good husband. I want a kind husband. You say you have integrity and strength. How do I know that? You must allow me to discover the truth myself. You need to allow me to develop trust. And that will take time. You must give me time to prove you are indeed a good man, a strong man, not a liar or a cheat." She pressed her lips together to stop them from trembling. "I understand that my family owes your family something. But I think you owe *me* something."

"You will have my wealth, and more riches than you can imagine."

"I don't want riches! Money doesn't buy happiness." Her fist went to her chest. "And I want happiness. This last year has been awful. Damien didn't break me, but he broke my heart. He hurt me so badly and I'm not ready for more pain."

"So what do you want?"

"Hope," she whispered. "I want hope."

"I don't understand."

"I want to believe that if this…marriage…is not good for me, if you are not good for me, you will set me free."

He said nothing. She could tell she'd surprised him. Caught him off guard.

"I cannot spend my life here in Saidia an unhappy hostage. I can't imagine you'd want such a woman for your wife, either. For that matter, I can't imagine your mother would want you to make your wife so terribly unhappy."

"Do you know anything of my mother?" he asked, his voice sharp.

She shook her head. "No."

"Then maybe it's time you learned who I am, and where I've come from. Follow me."

Jemma trailed after Mikael as he exited the courtyard. They traveled through a maze of hallways. Every time she was sure he'd turn right, he turned left. When she anticipated him turning left, he went right. The Kasbah halls seemed to be circular. It made no sense to her.

Finally he stopped in a spacious hall topped with a skylight and opened the tall door. "This is my personal wing," he said. "It includes a bedroom, office and living room, so I can work when here, should I need to."

She followed him through the tall door into a handsome living room. Wooden panels had been pulled back from the trio of windows and sunlight flooded the room, making the pair of low sapphire velvet couches glow and the gold painted walls shimmer.

They continued through the living room into another room, this one also bright with natural light as one entire wall was made of glass doors.

The room itself was sparsely furnished, the buff stone walls unpainted, and the plush carpet beneath her feet intricately woven of pale gold, faded blue, and a coral pink.

A low couch was on one side of the room while an enormous dark wood desk inlaid with pearl dominated the other side, positioned to face glass doors with the view of a spacious, but Spartan courtyard.

He crossed the floor to the desk, opened a drawer, and drew out a small jeweled picture frame. He held the frame out to her. "This is my mother at twenty-three, just two years younger than you are now."

She took the frame from him. The woman was young and blonde and very beautiful. She had straight bangs and high, elegant cheekbones. Her long hair hid one shoulder and her blue eyes were smiling, laughing, up at the camera.

"She's…so fair," Jemma said, brows tugging as she studied the laughing beautiful girl with straight white-blonde hair.

"She was American."

Jemma's head jerked up. Her gaze met his.

He nodded once. "Your mother was descended from a Mayflower family. So was my mother. She was American as apple pie."

Jemma felt a lump grow in her throat. She looked back down at the photo, noting the girl's swimsuit and cover up and the blue of the sea behind her. "Where was this taken?"

"The Cote d'Azur. My father met her when she was on holiday with friends in Nice. My father swept her off her feet. They were married within months of meeting."

"She's so beautiful."

"She was young and romantic and in love with my father… as well as in love with the idea of becoming Saidia's queen."

Jemma handed the framed photo to him. He put it back in the drawer. "My father betrayed her trust," he said quietly. "And then your father betrayed her trust. Which is why I promise you, I will not betray you. I am a man of my word. And if I vow to provide for you properly, I will. Over time our marriage will hopefully heal the rift between families and countries. It won't be immediate. It might not even happen in our generation, but I hope that it will be better for our children." He studied her, expression fierce, resolute. "We begin our journey as husband and wife tonight, by sharing our first meal together in the Bridal Palace."

Jemma's throat ached. She felt close to tears. "Would your mother approve of what you're doing?"

"Leave her out of this."

"How can I?" she choked. "You don't!"

"One day you will understand the importance of honor. One day when we have our children—"

"No!"

"That is fair. You are right. I will save the talk of children for later. Instead let us focus on tonight, and how we shall retreat to the Bridal Palace, for the first of our eight nights. For the next eight nights, I will pleasure you."

"And what happens after that eighth night?" Jemma asked tartly. "Do you disappear into your suite? Return to Buenos Aires? What happens then?"

"You are in control for the next eight nights. You get to pick a different pleasure each evening, or the same pleasure, or…no pleasure."

She frowned, not understanding.

He saw her expression, correctly reading her confusion. "According to Saidia law, the first eight nights are the groom's. The next eight nights are the bride's. The Saidia bride doesn't have to take her husband into her room, or her bed, for any of the next eight nights, unless she wants to. What happens during the second eight nights is entirely her choice."

"What is the point of that?" Jemma asked.

"It was to teach a randy bridegroom not to be selfish in bed, and provide an incentive for the groom to be patient and tender with his new bride, pleasuring her so thoroughly that she'll hunger for her husband's touch."

Jemma's cheeks were on fire again. Heat coursed through her, her skin prickled, suddenly almost too sensitive.

Mikael's dark eyes met hers. "And I assure you, I intend to

please you so thoroughly you'll beg me to return to your bed for every night of your eight nights."

She drew a slow breath, head spinning. Everything inside of her felt tight, tense.

"I have never heard of any honeymoon being so purely... carnal and erotic."

"It might sound like that, until you remember that most royal brides brought here were innocent virgins, carried here against their will. As I told you, it was customary for the royal groom to kidnap a bride from one of the rival desert tribes. The honeymoon was his chance to win his bride's affection, and loyalty, before he took her home with him. But, if he couldn't win her affections by the end of the sixteen days, then she could leave him without repercussions or shame."

That last bit caught Jemma's attention. "She could choose to go home?"

"If he couldn't make her happy in their sixteen days together." He reached out, stroked the sweep of her cheekbone, making her skin tingle. "I will please you," he said, quietly, decisively. "I promise to satisfy you completely."

She stared at him, wide-eyed, heart pounding. She'd loved Damien and she'd been quite sure Damien had loved her, but he'd never been overly concerned with pleasing her. Pleasuring her.

She couldn't quite get her head around the idea that Mikael was promising to satisfy her completely.

Sexually.

Fulfilling her every fantasy.

"You are making a lot of promises," she said unevenly, her mouth drying.

"They are promises I fully intend to keep."

"I worry that you are...unrealistic."

His hard expression softened. Amusement glimmered in his eyes. "I worry that your expectations are too low." His lips curved faintly. "Perhaps it's time I show you the Kasbah? This is no ordinary desert palace. Its outer walls hide a secret palace."

"A secret palace?" She looked at him, intrigued. "What does that mean? That there's a palace within the palace?"

"Yes. That is exactly what I do mean. Would you like to see? I can take you on a tour of the Bridal Palace now if you're interested."

The Bridal Palace? Was that its real name? Her eyebrows arched. "I'm very interested."

He smiled. "Good. We will start the tour with the rooms near your suite."

CHAPTER SEVEN

THEY LEFT HIS rooms, and walked through the maze of halls and corridors with Mikael giving her the history of the palace as they returned to her wing. "This Kasbah is known in Saidia as the Bridal Palace. For hundreds of years this is where the king of Saidia brought his new bride after the wedding ceremony. It is where the royal couple honeymoons, and where the king or prince would introduce his virgin bride to the pleasures of the marriage bed."

Mikael pointed down one hall, which led to the entrance of the Kasbah. "The bride would arrive, and pass through the same entrance you passed through last night, and then be escorted by her new maids to this wing. On arrival, the bride would be bathed, massaged with fragrant oils, then robed and taken to the first chamber, the white chamber—a room hidden off your room—which historically has been called the Chamber of Innocence. In the Chamber of Innocence, the groom claims his bride, consummating the marriage. In the morning, the bride is transferred to a different suite.

"Here," he added, walking down another hall to a different corridor and taking a turn to the right. "This is the Emerald Chamber." He opened the only door in the corridor and stepped back to let her have a look. "This is where the bride and groom spend their second day."

Jemma carefully moved past him to glance around the room. The walls were glazed green, the floor was laid with green and white tiles. The bed was gold with green silk covers and a dozen gold lanterns hung from the ceiling.

"There's a courtyard attached," he said. "The garden is fantastic, and the pool looks like a secret grotto."

They stepped out of the room, into the hall. They walked in a circular pattern, continuing right, down another hall to another door. "The Amethyst Room," he said, and it was a room of purple and gold, even more luxurious and exotic than the Emerald Chamber.

"There are eight rooms like these," Mikael said. "In this section of the Kasbah, the rooms have all been laid out in the shape of a large octagon, with a shared garden in the center. Some of the rooms also have a private courtyard, too. Each of the rooms are significant because they represent a different sensual pleasure."

He'd just opened a door to the Ruby Chamber but she didn't even look inside. She stared at Mikael, stunned, and fascinated. "Seriously?"

He nodded. "Each suite has a pleasure attached, and it varies from a form of sex, to a particular position."

Jemma blushed, suddenly very warm. "You're making this up."

"Not at all. Each night for eight consecutive nights, the groom takes his bride to a new room, initiating her into new carnal delights, teaching her, pleasuring her, as well as ensuring she knows how to pleasure him."

Her face burned, hot. It was almost as if a fire had been lit inside of her and she didn't know if it was the things he was saying, or his tone, but his words created erotic pictures in her head, pictures that were so intimate and real that she could scarcely breathe.

He led her around to each of the eight suites, and she marveled at each. The Bridal Palace was beyond fantasy. It was magical. Jemma felt as if she'd entered another world. A world she couldn't have imagined existed anywhere. And yet it did. *Here.*

The exotic perfection was almost too much to take in, each suite more spectacular than the last, the rooms splashed with jeweled color—violet, sapphire, gold, ruby, turquoise, emerald, and silver. The chambers were connected by tall columned corridors, the white and gold tiles shimmering at all hours of the day, while in the very center was a luxurious walled garden featuring pools, fountains, and exotic red, gold and ivory mosaic tiled pavilions.

She'd thought her courtyard was lovely, but the Bridal Palace's secret courtyard was so lavish and sensual it stole her breath, and made her heart hurt.

She didn't know why the Bridal Palace's sensual beauty created pain. She was certain it'd been designed to delight.

"You're very quiet," the sheikh said, turning to look at her.

She passed a small waterfall that tumbled and splashed into a deep bathing pool. "I'm in awe," she said, thinking this was the kind of place you wanted to be on your honeymoon. The low beds covered with the softest cotton and banked with silk cushions. The fragrant garden both hid and revealed the various gleaming pools.

This was a place for passion. Pleasure. Here anything seemed possible…

"I've never seen anything like this before," she added, voice unsteady. "It takes my breath away. These rooms, the gardens, they're pure fantasy. I feel like I'm in a dream."

"I think that's the point," he said, leading her from the central courtyard, through a room shimmering with silver, to the outside hall. "The fantasy element is to help both bride and groom overcome their inhibitions. Here, everything is possible."

The door shut behind them and they were suddenly back in an ordinary hall, in an ordinary world.

She looked at the closed door, amazed by what they'd just left behind. "The rooms…your story…it's a fairy tale for adults."

"But it's not a fairy tale, or a story. It's real. Part of Saidia's culture and tradition. This is where every Saidia king has brought his bride for eight hundred years."

"Your parents came here?"

He nodded. "My father brought my mother here. And now I've brought you."

Jemma's mouth opened, closed. She couldn't think of a single thing to say. It was all too incredible...the exotic beauty, as well as the seductive nature of the Kasbah. Everything in this palace was hedonistic. Indulgent. And he was using the promise of pleasure to cast a spell over her.

"Tonight is the first of our sixteen nights here. For the next eight nights, I shall pick the pleasure, and then on the ninth night, it becomes your choice."

He was walking her back to her suite now, and Jemma was glad he was leading. She felt dazed. Lost. Caught up in the most impossible dream.

"Not tonight," she said as they reached her door. "I'm not ready."

"A kidnapped bride is never ready," he said, and yet he was smiling to soften his words. "I also am not insensitive to the strangeness of our situation. I understand you have fears, and misgivings, but I believe it is better to begin sooner than later. You will be less anxious once we know each other."

"But shouldn't that happen before physical intimacy?"

"The physical intimacy will bind us together. It is the act of physical love that distinguishes the relationship, separating us from others."

Jemma pressed her hands together, fingers locking. "One more day. *Please.*"

"But you had one day already. We had today."

"I slept most of it away!"

"Which should mean you are rested and refreshed for tonight." They'd reached the entrance to her suite of rooms. He gestured to her door. "Inside your room you will find several presents from me. You will receive more later. For the next eight days and nights I will shower you with gifts, jewels, and my undivided attention. I think you shall soon discover that these eight days and nights will be everything you ever dreamed…and more."

His gaze met hers and held, even as his words echoed in her head, making her nerves dance.

Everything you ever dreamed…and more.

Just like that the night crackled, the air hot and heavy, sultry in the exotic pavilion.

Mikael was so close that he made the hair on her nape rise and her skin prickle. All she could think about was the sheikh stretching his big powerful body out over hers. Blood rushed to her cheeks and she fought to control her breathing.

"You are awfully confident, Your Highness."

"We are married. Don't you think it's time you used my given name?"

"I do not feel married."

"That will change soon."

Jemma disappeared into her room, pulse racing. She turned from the door and nearly tripped over the mountain of trunks stacked just inside the entrance to her sitting room.

The young maid was standing next to the trunks, smiling. "For you," she said. "From His Highness."

Jemma backed away from the trunks, panicked by the tower of gifts.

She didn't want presents. Didn't want to be showered with expensive gifts and jewels.

She wanted the life she had in London. She wanted her friends. Wanted her work. She wanted her own identity and freedom.

The maid watched Jemma, her dark eyes bright, expression cheerful and excited. "Shall I start your bath, Your Highness? We have much to do to prepare."

Jemma shook her head, feeling anything but excited. She couldn't do this. Couldn't go through with this. She wasn't the kind of woman who just gave up, who just gave in. She was not meant to be Mikael's queen. Her future was not here in Saidia, nor did she have any desire to bear the children that would heal the rift between families and countries.

"It is a very big day," the maid added carefully, her confident expression slipping, revealing the first hint of concern. "Much to do. Much tradition."

Jemma sat down on the edge of one of her low white sofas, her hands folding in her lap. "These are not my traditions."

The maid knelt next to Jemma. "Your Highness, do not be frightened. His Highness, Sheikh Karim, is a very good and powerful man. He is very fair. A man of his word. If he tells you something, it is so."

"I think you would say that about all Saidia kings."

"No. I would not say that about the last king, Sheikh Karim's father. The old king was not a good man. He made his first wife very sad. I think His Highness, Sheikh Karim, saw much as a boy. I think he saw things a child should not see. This is why he is different from his father. He has worked very hard to be a good king. The people love him. He honors and respects Saidia people, and Saidia tradition." The maid smiled. "The king will be good to you. You will be happy. I am already happy for you." Her hand indicated the trunks. "Already he has sent many gifts. He tries to show you already he is pleased with you. That you bring him honor."

Jemma shook her head. "He's trying to buy me."

The maid frowned. "Buy you? Like a camel?"

"Yes. But I'm not a thing to be bought."

"His Highness does not buy you. His Highness honors you. Gifts show respect. In Saidia, gifts are good things." She smiled more brightly. "Maybe now you look at your gifts, and then we get ready for tonight."

Jemma struggled to smile. "You open the trunks for me. Show me what is inside."

For the next several minutes, all the maid did was unpack the trunks, starting with the largest leather trunk on the bottom of the stack.

The biggest trunk was filled with clothes. Kaftans, skirts, sarongs, tunics, slinky evening gowns. The medium trunk contained shoes and heels and elegant jeweled sandals. The small trunk held jewelry and accessories.

There was one last trunk, but this one wasn't leather, but silver. The silver box's gleaming surface was embossed with elegant scrollwork and a jeweled handle. Jemma carefully unfastened the latches. Inside the silver box was a white garment bag, white shoes and a small, delicate white silk pouch.

"This is for tonight," the maid said, unzipping the garment bag to remove a long white satin gown that looked like something from a Hollywood movie. "Your bridal gown."

"My wedding gown?" Jemma corrected, thinking maybe she'd misunderstood the girl's English.

"No. The honeymoon gown. For pleasure." The maid smiled, her cheeks pink. "Tonight is the first night. You go to him in white. You meet him in the Chamber of Innocence."

"How do you know all this?"

"I come from the same tribe as Sheikh Karim. My mother and grandmother served the new Karim brides. And now I serve you. It is my job to prepare you for the king's pleasure."

Jemma was neither a virgin nor an innocent and yet she blushed, furiously, feeling ridiculously embarrassed, and shy. "I'm not sure about this."

"You don't need to worry. His Highness will know everything. He will teach you."

Jemma flushed again, her cheeks burning, trying not to feel mortified. The maid must think she was a timid virgin.

"Do you want to try it on?" the maid asking, admiring the long white satin gown.

"No." Jemma turned away from the gown, the fabric soft and begging to be touched, focusing instead on the remaining wedding night gifts and accessories. White satin shoes. Delicate white satin undergarments. And of course, the white silk pouch.

Curious, Jemma loosened the silver strings and emptied

the pouch into her hand. Glittering diamond and pearl earrings spilled into her palm. A small card slid out last, landing on top of the stunning diamond drop earrings.

My first gift to you. Please wear them tonight. I think they will look magnificent on you.

Jemma read the card twice, and then slowly exhaled, her heart hammering.

Was this really happening? Would she really go to him tonight, dressed like a virgin sacrifice, dazzling in diamonds and white?

Jemma slipped the earrings back into the silk pouch, and then placed the pouch and shoes inside the silver trunk before closing the lid and fastening it shut.

Yesterday afternoon she'd been in the middle of a photo shoot when Mikael arrived. She'd known nothing about him, and very little about Saidia, and yet now she was his wife, and being prepared for his bed.

She still couldn't wrap her head around it.

Jemma sat back on her heels and looked at the young maid. "Have you ever heard of a royal groom not satisfying his bride? Have you ever heard your mother or grandmother mention a kidnapped bride returning to her family? Has it happened in Saidia history before?"

The maid nodded. "Yes."

"A long, long time ago, or more recently?"

"During my great-great-grandmother's time, I think. Many, many years ago. And…" The maid chewed her lip, looking unsure of herself. "Maybe my mother's time."

Jemma frowned. "Your mother served my husband's mother."

"Yes."

"Mikael's mother was unhappy?"

"Not at first. Not during the honeymoon, but later."

"Why?"

She shrugged. "I do not know. My mother would never say."

The maid left to start Jemma's bath, and rather than argue with the maid about privacy, Jemma stripped her clothes off and spent the next half hour soaking in the deep marble tub, lost in thought.

The Kasbah was a palace within a palace, and Mikael descended from a line of royal men who'd been taught that it was necessary to know how to please a woman in bed, and even his *duty* to give his woman pleasure. But not just pleasure. He was expected to make her fall in love with him. She needed to want to stay in Saidia. She needed to be happy. And if, during the honeymoon, the Saidia groom couldn't make his bride happy, she could leave him after sixteen days.

The history fascinated Jemma. But it wasn't just history. They were facts. And the facts gave her pause.

If a Saidia man couldn't please his wife, he had to let her go.

Did that mean Mikael would let her go if he couldn't please her?

Out of the bath, the maid set to work rubbing exotic fragrant oils into Jemma's skin, and Jemma provided no resistance, lost in thought.

She'd been brought here as Mikael's first wife. But perhaps now she could force him to free her following their honeymoon. If she wasn't happy after eight days, she'd refuse him the next eight and demand to be allowed to return to her tribe.

While the oil dried, Jemma walked around the courtyard in her cotton kimono, letting the sun's warmth help her skin absorb the oil.

She knelt by the pool in the courtyard, and gazed down into the clear blue water, the bottom of the pool covered in cobalt blue tiles. Her face reflected back at her, her dark hair pulled back from her face, her expression appeared surprisingly serene in the water. Her calmness belied her resolve.

She would leave here.

She would not be charmed.

She would not fall in love.

She would not give him children.

What she'd give him were eight days and nights, and during those days and nights he'd have access to her body. But he'd never have her heart.

The maid fetched Jemma from the courtyard to do her hair.

Jemma's stomach churned as she sat at the silver dressing table, while the maid combed and twisted her hair into place, roping in strands of pearls and clusters of diamonds until Jemma's long dark hair was a glittering, jeweled work of art.

Was Mikael aware that he'd given her a way out? Did he know that she understood her freedom could be won?

But first she'd have to surrender to Mikael for eight days, and eight nights.

Could she do it?

Could she give herself to him totally? Handing over her body, her will, her need for control?

"Shall I help you with your dress now?" the maid asked, Jemma's hairstyle complete.

"No," Jemma said suddenly. She couldn't finish dressing, couldn't slip into the white satin gown, not until she'd seen Mikael. She needed to speak to him. She needed his promise that he'd honor Saidia tradition. "I need to go see His Highness, now. Will you please take me to him?"

The maid opened her mouth as if to protest and then nodded. "Yes, Your Highness. Please, follow me."

The maid knew the palace corridors and they walked swiftly from her wing to his.

The maid knocked on the outer door of Mikael's suite and then stepped back, discretely disappearing into the shadows.

Jemma drew a deep breath as she waited for the outer door to open. It did, and Mikael's valet gestured for Jemma to enter the king's suite.

Jemma glanced up into Mikael's central hall with the soaring ceiling topped by a skylight. She remembered the skylight and the second floor lined with balconies, reminding her of the New Orleans French Quarter.

"Looking for me?" Mikael's deep voice sounded behind her.

Jemma turned, blushing as she spotted Mikael in nothing but a snug white towel wrapped securely around his waist, revealing broad shoulders and muscular torso.

"Yes," she said, forcing her gaze from his impressive body up to his face. His black hair was damp, and glossy, his jaw freshly shaven. His gaze met hers and held.

Handsome, she thought, dazzled by the play of golden light over his bronze features. He was too handsome for his own good. No wonder he was arrogant.

"What can I do for you?" Mikael asked as his valet disappeared.

"We need to talk."

"And I thought you'd come to thank me for my gifts," he answered, smiling faintly.

"They are…lovely," she said hesitantly. "So yes, thank you. But—"

"But you want something else?" he interrupted.

She flushed. "Yes. You could say that."

His eyes, fringed by those endless lashes, narrowed. His gaze swept over her and even from across the courtyard she felt the heat in his eyes, felt the possession.

"What is it?" he asked.

Jemma grew hot. Her pulse quickened. She'd walked quickly the entire way from her room but it didn't explain this new heat in her veins. This was his fault. When he looked at her, he made her head light, made her feel ridiculously dizzy and weak. "I want something that isn't a physical gift."

"You don't care for jewels and clothes?"

"They're fine, but not my favorite gifts."

"I thought every woman loved jewelry and exquisite clothes."

"I am sorry to disappoint you."

He circled her slowly. "You don't disappoint me. You intrigue me. I'm intrigued right now. What it is that you want so badly you'd race to my room just an hour before we are to disappear into the Chamber of Innocence?"

Mikael watched color sweep Jemma's cheeks. She was beautiful in the pink kimono robe, and she sounded breathless and all he could think of was peeling the thin fabric from her shoulders and kissing the pale skin at her collarbone.

She had a beautiful body. He wanted her body. He wanted her.

"Would you care to sit?" he asked her.

"No. I think I'm better standing."

"Does what you need to say require courage?" he asked, wondering if she knew how beautiful she was. He doubted it. She was surprisingly modest. She had no airs or attitude. Someone in her family had done a good job raising her.

"It depends on how you'll take it," she answered.

"Then perhaps let's not talk now. Tonight is special. Tonight is about pleasure."

"Tonight cannot happen without us speaking, Your Highness."

He sighed, an exaggerated sigh. The sigh was purely for show. He was playing with her, enjoying her fire. "*Laeela*, I confess I'm not pleased with the direction our relationship is taking. We do a lot of talking. Or more accurately, you do a lot of talking, and I seem to be doing a great deal of listening."

"You're wrong, Your Highness. You actually never listen."

"I'm sure that's not right. It seems like you talk a great deal."

"That's maybe because you're not used to a woman who has a brain and wants to use it."

"I see." It required effort not to give in to the smile. "That might explain it, but I'm wondering if talking now will maybe interfere with our pleasure tonight? Perhaps we should wait and talk later."

"Most men probably never want to talk, Your Highness, but we must."

"Fine. You talk, and I will listen, provided there is no more of this Your Highness when we are in private. You're my wife, about to come to my bed. I understand you must call me Your Highness in public, but we are alone at the moment, and my name is Mikael."

She blinked and wet her lips, her face awash in rosy color, her eyes a brilliant green in her lovely face, flashing fire.

"Now, what is it you had to say?" he added, reaching out to touch her pink cheek.

She just looked at him with wide green eyes and he savored the moment. "What is it?" he persisted. "Tell me."

She drew a quick breath. "I want you to make me a promise."

She was negotiating with him. Interesting. "Yes?"

"I want you, as the king and leader of the Saidia people, to promise me that you will honor Saidia tradition, and the custom of your tribe."

He could see from the tilt of her chin that she expected him to fight her. She expected a problem. She was preparing to battle.

"I always try to honor Saidia tradition," he said.

"Then promise to honor this tradition."

"Perhaps you need to tell me what it is, first."

She looked into his eyes and then away. She seemed to struggle to find the right words, and then she shrugged, and blurted, "If you cannot make me happy in the first eight days and nights of our honeymoon, I want you to promise to send me home, to my family. My people."

She'd shocked him. For a moment he could think of nothing to say.

"During the tour you explained why the honeymoon is so important," she continued. "It made sense to me, and it made me respect your culture more. I am grateful you come from a culture that believes a woman should be happy, because I, too, believe a woman should be happy. I believe all women should be happy, just as I believe all women should have a say in their marriage, and future." She drew another quick breath. "*I* need to have a say in my future. I need my voice heard. You must give me my voice back."

"But you have your voice. I hear you quite plainly."

"Then give me a gift I will cherish, the gift of your word. Promise me I will be free to return home if you cannot make me happy."

"You doubt me?"

"I won't if you promise me I can trust you."

"I've told you my word is law."

"Then say to me, 'Jemma, if you aren't happy in eight days, I will put you on a plane, and send you back to London.'" Her green eyes held his. "That is all you have to do, and I will believe you, but I need a promise from you, or it is impossible to give you my body, or my heart, if I'm afraid, or full of fear and doubt."

He said nothing.

"Mikael," she added more softly, persuasively, "I need to know that I can trust you. I need to believe you will take care of me. Your promise is the gift of dignity and honor. Your promise means I feel safe and respected, and that gives us the basis for a future. Otherwise, we have nothing. And how can you build a future on nothing?"

She was like a queen, he thought, watching her. Beautiful and regal. Proud, slender, strong. With her dark hair and stunning green eyes, she could easily be one of the great Egyptian queens. Cleopatra. Nefertiti. Ankhesenamun.

If they had met under different circumstances, he would have made her his lover or mistress. He would have enjoyed spoiling her with gifts. He liked to spoil his woman, liked to please her. But he didn't love. He didn't want to love. Love complicated relationships. Love wasn't rational.

He was determined to be rational. He was determined to be a good king.

She reached toward him, her hand outstretched. "Mikael, I need to know you have not just your best interest at heart, but mine, too."

He stiffened. "As king I have all my people's best interests at heart."

"As my *husband,* you must have mine, too."

"I do."

Her hand lightly settled on his chest. "Then promise me, and I can meet you tonight with calm, and confidence, and *hope*."

He glanced down at her hand where it rested so lightly on his chest, just above his heart.

He captured her hand in his, holding her small fist to his chest. His thumb swept her wrist. He could feel the wild staccato of her pulse. She was afraid. He didn't like her fear. "You've no need to be afraid."

"That is not the same thing as a promise."

"You are still getting to know me, but you will discover I am a man of my word. I do not make rash promises, nor do I break my commitments."

She bit her lip and looked at him from beneath her long dark lashes. "So what does that mean?"

"It means I have eight days to make you happy."

He could see her bite down harder, her pink lip turning white in the center, where her teeth pressed into the tender flesh.

He both envied and pitied the spot.

Once she was completely his, he would suck and lick that poor lip to make amends. His body hardened in anticipation. He would very much like to suck and lick all of her. He would like to feel her tighten beneath him, and then shatter. "But I also understand your mistrust of men. Your father abandoned you, and then your fiancé did the same. You've been surrounded by men who only think of themselves, making rash promises, which is why I can safely give you my word that I *will* make you happy."

"And yet, if you cannot, you will let me return to London?"

His dark gaze raked her, appreciating the jut of breasts and swell of hips beneath the thin kimono. "Yes."

CHAPTER EIGHT

BACK IN HER room, Jemma couldn't look at herself as she stepped into the beautiful fitted white satin gown. It was too soft and sensual to be a wedding gown, and yet the slinky satin somehow managed to give the impression of a long and Western style bridal gown. The wedding night without the traditional wedding ceremony.

She sucked in a nervous breath as the maid fastened the dozens of tiny hooks in the back of the long dress, and then with shaking hands, she attached the diamond and pearl earrings to her earlobes.

She couldn't believe how her stomach flip-flopped as she stepped into her white-beaded silk shoes. Designer shoes. They fit like a glove.

Jemma glanced at herself in the dressing table mirror. She looked like a bride dressed for the bedroom.

And wasn't that exactly what she was? She was being prepared for her husband's bed. Oiled and scented and bejeweled for his pleasure.

But earlier, in his room, when he'd taken her hand, she hadn't felt fear. She'd actually liked the way his touch made her feel. He was strong and warm and it was such a small thing, this linking of fingers, and yet significant. Touch was powerful. His touch was surprisingly comforting.

And now she was curious about tonight. But not afraid.

Mikael arrived at Jemma's suite of rooms at eight o'clock and he watched her cross the sitting room floor, as she moved toward him, her head high, her eyes wide, the large diamond teardrops swinging from her earlobes, the brilliant cuts in the stone casting tiny dancing lights in every direction. Her gown molded to her body, the delicate straps and cups of the dress revealing smooth shoulders and the swell of her breasts before hugging her flat tummy and the lush curve of her hips and butt.

His narrowed gaze slid over her tall, slender body, appreciating how the satin caressed her, and yet he could also see her without the luscious satin, remembering that stunning glimpse of her when she'd dropped the fur coat during the shoot, and how the full shape of her breasts had been revealed.

The impact of her physical beauty had shocked him. He'd had such a visceral reaction there on the sand dune. He'd been furious—outraged—but he'd also felt a wave of pure possession.

Mine, he'd thought.

He'd wanted to cover her. Take her away from everyone. He'd told himself it was duty, responsibility, a response to a wrong.

Now he wondered if it was more than that.

Mine.

He held out his hand to her. She gave him her hand. It was shaking. He took her hand, his fingers lacing with hers.

He lifted her hand to his mouth, just as he had earlier, but this time he kissed the back of each finger. "Eight days and nights."

"And it all starts now?"

"Yes."

He swung her into his arms then and carried her down the connecting halls until they reached the entrance to the Bridal Palace.

"We are here," he said, pushing the door open and carrying her inside to a room that glowed with hundreds of white candles.

Jemma spotted the bed, surrounded by more candles, and looked the other way. "Are we going to bed now?"

"No." His deep voice sounded amused. "I'm starving. Haven't eaten since our late lunch. Wouldn't you prefer a bite to eat first?" he asked, setting her on her feet.

"Yes," she said quickly. "Please."

Mikael took her hand and led her past the dozens of candles illuminating the immense bed, to the opposite side of the room, where a door opened to a private courtyard fantastically transformed into a tropical garden with a manmade grotto and splashing waterfall. Dozens of candles lined the walkway, and more candles outlined the steps to the grotto and door.

It was warm in the garden, and fragrant with orchids and lilies and Mikael pulled her close to his side as he led her along the narrow path lined with candles, down an even more narrow stone staircase to a secret room inside the grotto where a table had been set for them among a sea of pale blue silk cushions.

The grotto was made entirely of stone and illuminated with a dozen blue glass lanterns that hung from the pale ivory stone ceiling. Water lapped in a small pool while above them came the sound of rushing water tumbling through over the waterfall.

"This is unbelievable." Jemma breathed, taking a seat among the cushions, very aware of Mikael as he sat down next to her.

He'd come to her tonight not in traditional Saidia robe and head covering, but in black trousers and an elegant dress shirt and once seated at the table, he proceeded to roll the sleeves of his shirt back on his muscular forearms, and then open the shirt another button at the collar, revealing a hint of bronzed skin just below his throat.

"That's better," he said.

She swallowed hard. He'd shocked her earlier in the towel, but it was just as shocking to see him now in Western clothes. He didn't look like a sheikh. He just looked gorgeous.

He looked at her. "You don't think so?"

"No, you look…quite…good," she murmured, thinking good was a total understatement. He looked fantastic.

"Quite good," he repeated, lips curving slightly. "I will take that as a compliment coming from you."

"I'm sure you are complimented all the time. You must know you are very beautiful for a man."

He laughed then. It was the first time she'd ever heard him laugh, really laugh, and the flash of his straight white teeth against his bronzed skin, and the crinkle of his eyes made her heart race.

"I don't get complimented very often," he said.

"No? Why not?"

"I think people might be afraid to pay me compliments."

She arched a brow. "What do you do? Chop off heads?"

"No. But I have a reputation for being no-nonsense."

"I'm sorry to hear that."

His teeth flashed again but he said nothing else, and for the next hour staff came and went, bearing platters of food until the low table was covered. Chicken with tomatoes and honey. Lamb cutlets, tangy beef, coconut rice, a tagine of yam, carrots and prunes.

After the past several days of stress, Jemma was glad to just relax, and eat, and sip her wine. Mikael was his most charming tonight. During dinner he told her stories, amusing stories. "You said earlier you're not a fan of jewels and clothes," he said, leaning against the cushions. "So what do you like? Art? Antiques? Cars?"

"Books." She could see she'd surprised him. "I love to read."

"Fiction?"

"Fiction, non-fiction, everything. Although when I was a girl, I only wanted to read romances. My mother was convinced I'd run off and join the circus or something equally risky and foolish."

"What will she think when she discovers you've married me?"

"She'll be horrified."

He didn't seem to like that. "Why?"

"Because our cultures are too different and she'd be worried that I'd be trapped in a life where I couldn't be myself, and the lack of freedom would make me desperately unhappy."

"That's quite specific."

"Morgan's short, unhappy marriage made quite an impression on all of us."

"And yet the day of her wedding she seemed ecstatic."

"Exactly. But Morgan was so infatuated with Drakon that she didn't ask any hard questions about what her life would be like in Athens, and their marriage was a shock for her. She ended up bitterly unhappy as a new bride in a new city and their relationship quickly fell apart." Jemma smoothed a wrinkle from her satin skirt. "Mother had warned her that life in Greece, as the wife of a Greek shipping tycoon wouldn't be easy, not for an independent American girl who is accustomed to making decisions for herself. And so I'm quite sure my mother would be even more upset if I turned around and married a Saidia sheikh."

Mikael said nothing for a long moment. "Even if it improves your situation?"

It was Jemma's turn to fall silent.

"I'm aware your brother is the only Copeland who has any financial assets left," Mikael added. "And the only reason he does, is because he lives in Europe, and his assets couldn't be seized, but your government will go after him. What he hasn't yet lost due to scandal, will soon be taken by your government."

"Maybe it won't happen," she said, not really believing it herself.

He gave her a skeptical look. "Isn't that the same thing you said about your mother's home? And didn't the government just take that?"

Jemma drew a short breath. It had been one thing losing

the house on St. Bart's and the lodge in Sun Valley, but it was painful losing one's childhood home. Jemma had lived in the Greenwich house from the time she was six until she'd left for London. And maybe she didn't live at home any longer, but it was still her home. It was where she liked to picture her mother, where they all came together to celebrate Christmas or a special occasion.

The government shouldn't have taken the house a month ago. It was her mother's, from the divorce. But apparently her father's name was on the title, too, and that was all they needed to seize it.

"It's not been easy for my mother, no," Jemma said roughly, unable to look at him, the pain fresh and sharp all over again. "But she's lucky she has a few friends who have stood by her. She's relying on their kindness now."

Jemma didn't tell the entire truth.

Yes, a few friends had stood by her mother. But the rest had dropped her. The majority had dropped her. Just like most of Jemma's friends had disappeared, too. It happened to her sisters as well. She had no idea if her brother, Branson, was abandoned. He'd never talked about it, even though he, too, lived in London. But then, Branson never revealed anything personal. He'd always been private and self-contained, so self-contained, that Jemma hadn't been comfortable going to her brother this year and asking for help, or a loan, or even a friendly ear. Instead she'd struggled to handle it all—the shame from her father's duplicity, and the pain of being rejected by the man she loved more than life itself.

She felt Mikael's fingers on her cheek. She stiffened and drew back, then realized he'd touched her because he was wiping away tears. Her tears.

She hadn't even realized she was crying.

"I'm sorry," she whispered, turning away to hide her face.

He turned her face back to him and gently swept his thumb across her right cheek, and then her left. His expression was troubled. Brooding. "Do you cry for your mother?"

"Yes."

"Just your mother? Or, perhaps you are also still hurting from that spineless Englishman who calls himself a model?"

She made a soft, rough sound. "He's a great model."

"But a lousy man."

She smiled despite herself, and then her smile faded. "My sister Logan said he did me a favor. She said it was better that I find out who he is now, before we married, instead of after."

"Your sister is right." His thumb slid across her cheekbone, and then down, along her smooth jaw, his attention fixed now on her mouth. He was going to kiss her. She was sure of it, she could tell by the expression in his eyes, and the way the air sparked and crackled around them, tense, and electric.

She felt raw and emotional. Confused. Everything was changing; the energy between them was different. He'd been so harsh and cold in the beginning but he was different now. He seemed as if he might care.

His head dipped. Her tummy flipped. Her pulse raced. His mouth almost touched hers, but didn't. His breath caressed her lips. "I am sorry that spineless Englishman hurt you. I am also sorry that I add to your pain."

Her heart squeezed. She struggled to catch her breath, feeling bruised.

"But I will make you happy, *laeela*. I promise."

She stared into his eyes, lost, dazzled.

"You will enjoy being my wife." He stroked her cheek again. "You will have riches beyond compare."

Jemma exhaled hard, and sat back, the magic gone.

He didn't understand her. He didn't understand that what she wanted, *needed*, had nothing to do with wealth. "Money does not buy happiness. I've no desire for riches, or wealth. I've had both, and money can buy things, but not what my heart needs."

"What about your body?"

"My *body*?"

His dark eyes gleamed. "What about what your body needs?"

"I don't understand."

"Who worships your body?"

Without wanting to, she thought of Damien. They'd had a good relationship, and great sex, but she wouldn't say Damien ever worshipped her body. She'd never had a boyfriend who'd worshipped her body, and had begun to think after conversations with her girlfriends, that few men did. "No man worships a woman's body."

"I fully intend to worship your body."

"This is incredibly uncomfortable. Perhaps it's time we discussed your body."

Mikael grinned. Like his laugh earlier, it was the first time she'd really seen him smile, a real smile and his teeth flashed again, and a tiny dimple appeared on the right side of his mouth. It was astonishing. Not just because he'd smiled, but because of what it did to his face. The smile transformed his hard, fierce features. He looked so approachable, so appealing.

She sucked in a breath, dazzled. "You shouldn't do that, you know."

A hint of a smile lingered at the corners of his mouth. "Do what?"

"Smile."

"Why not?"

"It makes you seem almost human."

"I *am* almost human."

"I had no idea," she retorted, trying to ignore the thumping of her heart and the way he made desire coil inside her.

He smiled again, and his expression was so warm and playful that she suddenly wanted more of him.

Wanted him closer. Wanted him kinder. Wanted him to be good to her.

"I like how fierce you get," he said.

"You deliberately provoke me."

The dimple deepened at the corner of his mouth. "Maybe."

In that moment she saw who he might have been had his life turned out differently. Or perhaps, this is how he might have been with her from the start, had she not been Jemma Copeland.

Maybe he really was warm and sexy, charming and engaging. Maybe.

"And my body is very fine," he said, the smile still lingering in his eyes. "I appreciate your concern."

Suddenly, she very much wanted to know more about him, who he was, and how he lived. Did he have lots of women in his life? Was he the kind of man who serial dated or did he prefer having a long-term relationship?

"Tell me about your body," she said, trying to sound offhand. "Does it see a lot of action?"

"I don't think that's appropriate."

"I'm not asking you to divulge names or numbers. I just want to know you. I'm curious about you. It's the sort of thing a woman wants to know about her man." She held his gaze. "So, are you a player?"

"I used to be a player. I'm not anymore. I haven't been for a couple years."

"Why?"

"Age? Maturity? I just know that around thirty I started to get tired of the chase, and would have just one relationship at a time. How about you?"

"I like having a boyfriend, but don't need to be in a relationship. I'm picky. I would rather be with no one than just anyone."

"A woman with high standards."

"A woman that prefers books to casual sex."

"You might just be the perfect kidnapped bride."

There was silence for a minute and Jemma felt a thousand different things.

But then from the first time she'd met Mikael, he'd made her feel a lot. And here, in this…pleasure palace…she'd begun to feel the whisper of a craving for something. She wasn't sure what it was she wanted, but her dreams last night had stirred something within her and all day she'd felt a restlessness and an ache.

Like a craving for sensation.

Staring into his eyes, she was teased by the possibility. Teased by the suggestion of pleasure. It would feel so good to feel good again. To feel like a woman again. To feel close to someone again.

"If you've finished your dinner," Mikael said rising. "It's time to come with me."

They climbed the stairs from the grotto's secret room to the courtyard of fragrant white lilies and vines clinging to rock. White candles still glimmered against the walls and outlined the walkway. But now in the middle of the courtyard, between the waterfall and door to the Chamber of Innocence stood a narrow table covered in crisp white sheets.

Jemma looked at Mikael, uncertain. "What is that?"

"A massage table. I'm going to give you a massage," he said. "You'll lie there, face down—"

"Why?"

"Most massages start with the back."

"Yes, but why are you giving me the massage?"

"I think you'd enjoy it. And it would help you relax. I want you to relax. I want you to realize that everything that will happen here in the Bridal Palace will feel good. I will never do anything you don't want. And if I do something that does make you uncomfortable, all you have to do is speak up." He drew the top sheet back on the table. "Any questions?"

Jemma tugged on her dress. "Do I wear this?"

"No. You'll take that off—everything off—and then lie down between the sheets, naked."

He'd turned around to give her privacy while she disrobed, but she was on the massage table now, tucked between the sheets.

He looked down at her on the table, her dark glossy hair tumbling over one shoulder.

The massage was for her, not him. He wanted her now. He wanted her naked in his bed now. But she wasn't ready, and he'd meant it when he told her that she had to be comfortable. She had to want him before anything would happen between them.

He placed his hands over the sheet covering her back, letting her feel the pressure of his hands, letting his hands warm her.

After a moment he smoothed his hands over the sheet covering her back.

She felt good. Warm, solid but smooth.

This wasn't going to be a sexual massage. He'd told her that before they started. It was to show her he could be trusted. He wouldn't hurt her, or force her to do anything she didn't want to do.

This massage was simply to help break the ice.

Develop awareness. Create ease between them. Stir the senses, too, so that she'd be comfortable with him physically. You couldn't impose desire. It must come from within.

He concentrated on learning the shape of her back through the sheet, the sheet protecting her, giving her a sense of safety. He had told her that at any point she could stop the massage. If at any point she felt uncomfortable or threatened, she just needed to speak up and the massage would end. But he didn't expect her to stop it.

Moving from her shoulders down, he ran his palms from her spine out, smoothing tension away, relaxing the muscles, letting her continue to warm, encouraging her to breathe more deeply.

After several minutes he drew the sheet down, folded it low on her hips, leaving her lovely back exposed. His eyes followed the line of her body, the narrowing of her waist to the soft swell of her hips. The sheet rested on her bottom, hiding the cleft of her cheeks, but again, he knew it was there. He wanted to see it. Touch it. Touch her.

And he would touch her, but not there, not today.

He drew her long hair into his fist, and quickly braided it, before draping the braid over her shoulder, leaving her back bare.

As he stepped away to reach for the oil he could see her profile. Her eyes were closed, her full lips softly parted. Her pale skin gleamed, and his gaze dropped to the side of her soft breast, and then lower to the gentle curve of hip.

He hardened. He'd wanted her for hours. He felt as if he lived in a constant state of arousal around her.

He'd desired many women, and knew how to pleasure his women, but this one made him ache.

Or maybe it was the fact that he couldn't have her, not today, or tomorrow, or even the day after that made him hurt.

Pouring warm oil into his hands, Mikael rubbed his palms together, spreading the oil, thinning it, and yet the slippery texture was so sensual that he wasn't sure he could do this. It was to tease her, but he was teasing himself and he hated it.

He placed his hands in the middle of her back, where he'd rested them a few moments ago when the sheet still covered her, and then he began to stroke her back, with smooth, firm deliberate strokes to relax her.

She was tense but he was patient, and as he worked on her back, he focused on the satin texture of her skin, the supple muscle beneath the skin, and the long elegant lines of her— shoulder, upper arm, spine, hip, thigh to calf.

For the next two hours he rubbed and kneaded, massaging every muscle group, working on her back, and then massaging her front, her arms, shoulders and the upper planes of her chest. Aware of the stiff peaks of her nipples beneath the loosely draped sheet his own body tightened in response. He wanted her.

He would wait until she gave herself to him. Would wait until she asked—no, begged—for release.

His hands stopped moving. He leaned over her, whispered that he was done, and told her to hold the sheet.

She did, and he scooped her up, carrying her into the Chamber of Innocence where he laid her in the big bed.

"Good night," he said, smoothing the hair back from her forehead. "Sleep well. I will see you in the morning."

He'd carried her into the bedroom and then left her.

Jemma rolled over onto her tummy, and pressed her face into the pillow, her body aching.

She ached for more. Ached to be filled, satisfied.

Hopefully she wouldn't have to lie here like this tomorrow night feeling so...tense. Frustrated. It wasn't a good feeling. Hopefully tomorrow it would be different. Hopefully tomorrow she'd sleep contented. Because wasn't that the sheikh's promise? He was to fulfill her needs, give her pleasure?

Yes, the massage had been nice.

She'd very much enjoyed being rubbed and stroked with warm fragrant oils.

And he'd been a great masseuse, the best she'd ever had. He'd been extremely thorough, taking his time, making the massage last for hours. But that was the trouble.

The massage was supposed to be the start of something. A preliminary to foreplay. She'd expected more. The feel of his fingers working knotted muscles, made her imagine his fingers doing other things...

She'd lay on the massage table knowing that soon he'd touch her, and it wouldn't be just relaxing, but exciting. Stimulating.

She couldn't help daydreaming during the massage, couldn't help fantasizing.

She'd entertained the fantasies, too, because surely she'd need them for the next thing. Sex.

But there had been no next thing.

Just the deliciously long massage by a man who obviously had quite a bit of expertise, and then a good-night.

Most cordial of him. If she'd gone to a spa she'd expect him to be waiting on the other side of the door with a lovely chilled glass of lemon water for hydration purposes. But she wasn't at a spa. She'd expected the massage to…deliver…

It hadn't.

The sheikh knew exactly what he was doing.

Turning her on, leaving her high and dry, leaving her wanting more.

Jemma would have something to say to Mikael Karim in the morning.

CHAPTER NINE

IT TOOK HER a long time to fall asleep the night before, and when she woke in the morning, it took her a long time to want to leave her bed.

The massage hadn't just stirred her body, it'd somehow stirred her emotions. She woke up feeling unsettled. Undone.

Mikael had promised her that he'd make her happy in their eight days together, but she felt far less comfortable and optimistic now than she had yesterday before he'd carried her across the threshold of the Chamber of Innocence.

But maybe it was this room, she thought, her gaze sweeping the white marble chamber. It was too formal and too cold.

Too lonely, too.

She hadn't imagined that the eight nights of pleasure would start with her sleeping alone. She understood why he'd done it—he was trying to put her at ease—but it was isolating here in this room. The cold marble and silk panels might appeal to someone else, but not to her.

She grabbed her pillow and hugged it. She suddenly missed her family very much and that was saying something because Jemma had been independent for years.

When she'd moved to London at eighteen, her sister Victoria had teased her, saying Jemma would never last in London, and predicted that she would be back within a matter of weeks.

Victoria was wrong. Jemma had never returned, and it had actually been surprisingly easy to leave her family. Maybe it was because as the youngest, she'd grown up watching the others move on and move out. By the time she'd reached her teens, it was just her, and her mom, and her mom was ready for freedom, too.

And London had been a good fit. Once Jemma had moved there, she'd found it easy to embrace her new life, seizing every opportunity, taking every decent job, whether home or abroad. She liked to travel, was comfortable in hotel rooms, didn't mind the long hours, either. Being the youngest, and having to learn to entertain herself, proved beneficial. Jemma was self-reliant. She told herself she needed nothing, and no one.

But that wasn't true, either.

Of course she needed people. She needed good people, loving people, people who wouldn't abandon her the moment things got difficult.

A knock sounded on her door and it opened to reveal Mikael, dressed in casual khaki trousers and a white linen shirt, with a scrap of hot orange fabric in his hands.

"For you," he said, carrying the sheer tunic to her where she lay in bed.

She blinked at him, this new him, still finding it difficult to reconcile the intimidating sheikh with this very sexy man who looked as if he'd be incredibly comfortable without anything on.

Her hands shook as she unfolded the tunic. The neckline was again jeweled and bundled in the center was a tiny blood-orange bikini.

"We're swimming?" she asked, lifting the bikini top, and noting that the silky cups looked very small.

"Only if you feel like it. We're having breakfast outside in the center courtyard, next to the pool. It's already hot today. You might want to swim." He gazed down at her. "You don't have to wear the suit, either. I wasn't sure how comfortable you'd feel swimming naked."

Heat rushed to her face. She grabbed the tiny bikini. "I'll wear the suit, thank you."

* * *

It was a very lazy, self-indulgent day. Jemma felt as if she were on holiday at a luxurious resort. She'd been in and out of the pool a couple times to cool off, but now she stretched out on a plush lounge chair, sunbathing, while Mikael lay on a lounge chair next to her, reading.

She couldn't help sneaking glances at him every now and then, astonished to see him in swim trunks. Astonished by his abs, and his long muscular legs, and the thick biceps. He was nothing like the sheikh she'd met three days ago. He seemed nothing like a sheikh at all.

She looked past him to the pool that sparkled in the sun. She could see one of the staff walking toward them with a tray of fresh chilled towels and more lemon flavored ice water, along with little cups of something.

The little cups contained sorbet, a delicious pineapple sorbet that Jemma ate with a tiny spoon. Mikael didn't eat his. But he sat up to watch her lick the melting sorbet from her spoon.

"You make me hungry," he said, his dark gaze hooded, his deep voice husky.

She blushed and pretended she didn't understand, but it was impossible not to understand what he meant when he stared at her mouth as if it were edible.

"You have a sorbet here," she said. "It's melting quickly, though."

"Perhaps I'll just pour it on you and lick it off."

A wave of heat hit her. She suddenly felt scorching hot. "You wouldn't."

"Don't tempt me."

She sucked the tiny bit of fresh pineapple from the tip of the spoon, assessing. "Where would you pour it?"

"You play with fire, *laeela*."

She squinted up at the sun. "It is hot out."

"Very hot," he agreed, his deep voice now a rumble.

Her tongue flicked at her upper lip, sweeping the sticky juice off. "Maybe you should get into the pool and cool off."

"Maybe you should stop eating your ice as if you were desperate to have sex." He saw her expression and shrugged. "Just a bit of friendly advice."

"You're trying to help me, are you?"

"Protect you."

She sucked hard on the little spoon before looking at him, winged eyebrow arching. "From whom?"

"Maybe from what," he replied, his dark gaze now sweeping her as if he could eat all of her from head to toe.

It was thrilling. Her pulse quickened and Jemma felt a little frisson of excitement race through her. "Which is…?"

"Ravishment."

"Ah." She swallowed hard, and pressed her thighs and knees together, suddenly finding it very hard to breathe normally.

She couldn't remember the last time being ravished sounded appealing. In fact, being ravished had never sounded appealing until now.

It was time something exciting happened. She'd sat here all morning in her tiny blood-orange bikini and wanted his attention. Now that she had it, she wasn't ready to lose it.

"Would it hurt?" she asked. "Being ravished?"

He considered her, his dark gaze raking her. "No," he said at length. "It'd feel very, very good."

Jemma squeezed her knees tighter. "How do I know? You've never even kissed me."

His eyes lit. His hard features shifted, his jaw growing harder even as his mouth curved. He looked dangerous and gorgeous.

She wanted him to pounce on her, devour her.

"Do you want me to kiss you?" he asked, his eyes so dark and hot and intense that she felt like the sorbet, melting into a puddle of sweet sticky juice.

She was almost twitching in her lounge chair. She felt so turned on and strung out at the same time. "Yes. But only if you kiss really, really well."

* * *

Mikeal hadn't planned on liking his new bride. He hadn't even wanted to like her. But she was growing on him. She was by turns smart, funny and fierce, and stunning whether in a formal gown, or a swimsuit by the pool.

She looked incredible right now, as a matter of fact, with her hair still damp from her last swim, her skin flushed and golden from the sun, her amazing body barely covered in that swimsuit which was the color of his desert at sunset.

He'd wanted her all morning but her provocative words threatened to push him over the edge.

She was such a tease. He liked it, though. He liked her fire, wanted to taste her fire. Flame it. Make her burn.

"If you're such a great kisser, why haven't you kissed me?" she asked, tossing her head, sending damp strands of hair over her shoulder to cling to the swell of her breast.

Desire and hunger shot through him. He ached. He hurt. But he would take this so slow that she would be the one begging for him.

His gaze swept over her, admiring the fullness of her breasts, her flat belly, and the bright silky fabric just barely covering her there, between her thighs.

His body tightened with arousal.

"If I start kissing you," he answered, his voice so deep it was almost a growl, "you wouldn't want me to stop."

"You're so conceited," she said, nose in the air, but squirming at the same time.

"I'm honest."

Her cheeks darkened to a dusty pink. "To me, it sounds like a boast. You talk a lot but do very little."

He loved that he could arouse her so easily. He could feel her humming now, wanting, needing. "You love to challenge me," he drawled.

"I was just saying—"

He snapped his fingers, interrupting her, and then pointed to his chair. "Come here."

Her green eyes darkened, widened. She swallowed hard.

"Come, big talker," he said. "Let's see how brave you really are."

And just like that, her courage failed. She ducked her head, bit her lip, uncertain and shy.

He hid his smile. He'd expected as much.

She was a tease. One of those good girls who wanted to be bad.

He stood up, crossed to her chair, and tugged her to her feet. Her green eyes flashed again, worry, excitement, uncertainty.

He held her by the wrist, led her into the red and ivory pavilion behind them, and drew the silk curtains closed, hiding them.

"Sit," he ordered.

She sat down on one of the low couches that wrapped the wall. He sat down next to her.

"What are we doing?" she whispered.

"Whatever we feel like doing," he answered, his head dipping, dropping low, his mouth so close she could feel the warmth of his breath against her skin.

Jemma held her breath, waiting for the kiss. She felt as if she'd been waiting forever for this moment. But he was taking his time, his lips lightly brushing across her cheek toward her ear.

She turned her head toward him, wanting his mouth on her mouth but his lips were exploring the high curve of her cheekbone, his lips a caress across her sensitive skin. Hot darts of pleasure shot through her. His mouth felt good on her. He smelled good, too. She wanted more of him, not less.

Jemma turned her mouth to his again, inhaling his scent, relishing the rich spicy fragrance of his skin. He'd shaved earlier, this morning, and his jaw was smooth and firm, his mouth full and so very sensual.

Promising pleasure.

Unable to resist, Jemma put her lips to his, and waited. Waited to see what he would do. Waited to see what would happen next.

If he intended to seduce her, she would let him do the work. She was in the mood to be seduced, too. Ready for pleasure, sensation, satisfaction. Exquisite satisfaction.

His hand moved to her chin, fingers trailing across her jaw in a leisurely exploration, and yet every little brush of his fingers made her insides tighten and squirm and her breasts, already aching, feel excruciatingly sensitive.

She wanted him to touch her there, on her nipples, and touch lower, between her thighs. She sighed, growing impatient.

"You're not happy?" he asked, against her mouth.

She squirmed as his fingers played with her earlobe, lightly circling the soft tender skin again and again, making her senses swim and her head spin. "This is a bit frustrating," she answered. "I think it's time you just kissed me."

His lips brushed hers again. "But I am kissing you."

"No," she said, arching as he found the hollow beneath her ear and did something delicious to it, so delicious that she clenched inwardly, craving his hard body filling her, warming her, satisfying her. "A proper kiss," she insisted, no longer caring that she was supposed to resist him. Somehow reality no longer mattered, not when need licked at her veins and Jemma felt starved for sensation.

She reached up to clasp his face, her hands learning the shape of his jaw, the hard angles and planes as she pressed her lips to his, deepening the kiss, focused only on the heat between them.

He drew back after a moment, his eyes almost black in the dark pavilion interior. "Maybe we should stop. I don't want to force you."

"I don't think you're forcing me," she said, giving her head a slight shake, as if to clear her head of the heat and need and intense physical craving to be touched. *Taken.*

She throbbed and pulsed in places that shouldn't throb and pulse. "If anything, I feel as if I'm forcing you."

The corner of his mouth lifted. "I'm not being forced. Trust me."

She stroked her hand over the warm hard plane of his face.

Such a beautiful face. He was using his good looks against her. His charm, too. "You're too good at this."

His laughter was a deep rumble in his chest. "That's better than being bad at this."

"You're making it impossible for me to resist you."

"But you can. All you have to do is say stop, and we are done. I will never force you to do anything."

Then his mouth traveled down her neck, over her collarbone, down her chest, to the swell of her breasts. He lips teased the underside of the breast through the fabric of her bikini, finding nerves in every place he touched. She shivered, gasping as his mouth settled over her taut nibble, sucking the tip through the fabric.

She arched as he sucked harder, the pressure of his mouth making her inner thighs clench together with need.

She was the one to tug the fabric away from her breasts, exposing her nipple, and she was the one to draw his head back down, so his lips covered her bare breast.

She sighed at the feel of his mouth on her hot skin. His lips were warm, the tip of his tongue cool, but once he took the tight bud of her nipple in his mouth, it was his mouth that felt hot, wet, and she gasped, arching into him, her hips lifting, grinding, her body on fire.

She wanted him to take her now. She wanted his hands between her thighs, peeling her bikini bottoms off, wanted him to part her knees and thrust deep into her body, filling her, making the maddening ache inside of her go away.

But he didn't go lower, his hands stayed at her breasts, his mouth fastened to her nipple, sucking and licking, drawing hard on her, whipping her to a frenzy. Throbbing, she rolled away from him, and sat up, stunned that he'd brought her to the verge of an orgasm. She would have climaxed, too, if she hadn't stopped him.

She could barely look at him, excruciatingly shy. The sensations inside her were still so intense. How could she climax without him even touching her between her legs?

Mikael turned her face to him. "Did I scare you?" he asked quietly, his dark eyes searching hers.

She shook her head, but there were tears in her eyes. Her emotions felt wild.

"What then?"

"You're just very good at all...that."

He stroked her cheek with his thumb. "It was too much."

Her eyes burned. Her throat squeezed. "I don't know you." His touch was soothing. It eased some of the tension within her, but not enough. "I don't know you," she repeated. "And for me to feel this way, physically, I think I should."

Jemma always found a way to surprise him.

But it wasn't her words that surprised him now, as much as her emotion. He felt her confusion. She didn't understand what she was feeling.

She wasn't who he thought she was. She was nothing like her father. And her softness and sweetness reminded him of his mother.

Suddenly, he wondered what his mother had been like, as a girl, before she'd married his father. She must have been daring and adventuresome. She was American, after all, and she'd married his father, a sheikh, and although she'd loved the exoticism of her husband's culture, she'd apparently never assimilated into the culture, and Mikael's father hadn't helped her adapt, either. He'd left her to fit in. Left her to sort it out for herself.

A mistake.

But then, their entire marriage had been a mistake. Even he had been a mistake.

His mother had said as much, too.

His chest grew tight, the air bottled inside his lungs.

He did not want his future to be like his past. He did not want his children to grow up with such terrible unhappiness.

He lifted Jemma's hand, kissed her palm, her wrist, feeling the flutter of her pulse against his lips. Her skin felt soft and warm. She was soft and warm and he felt the strongest urge to protect her.

"I have a gift for you," he said, leaning back on the cushions.

"I don't need gifts," she answered, still unsettled, still reserved. "In fact, material things just leave me cold."

"So how can I spoil you?"

"I don't want to be spoiled."

"What can I give you then?"

She studied him for a long moment. "I want to know about you. Tell me something about you."

"Me?"

"Rather than presents, every day tell me something new about *you*."

"Showering you in jewels would be easier."

"Exactly." She looked at him, her expression almost fierce. "So if you want to give me something meaningful, give me part of you. Let me know you. That would be a true gift…one *this* bride would treasure."

He smiled faintly. "What shall I tell you? What would you like to know?"

"Tell me more about your mom," she said promptly. "And your dad."

"That's not a very pleasant subject."

"Parents and divorces never are."

"So why would you want to know about them?"

"Because they're important people in our lives. Our parents shape us. For good, and for bad." Her gaze met his. "Were you closer to one than the other?"

He sighed. He didn't want to talk about this, he didn't, but he liked her lying here next to him. She felt good here, and he wanted her to stay. "I don't remember being close to my father," he said after a moment. "But I'm sure he doted on me. Saidia parents tend to spoil their children, especially their sons."

"And your mother?"

"Adored me." It was uncomfortable talking about his mother. "She was a good mother. But then they divorced."

"Do you know why they divorced?"

He looked at her. "Do you know why your parents divorced?"

"My dad was having an affair."

Mikael hated the heaviness in his chest. He reached out and touched a strand of her hair, tugging on it lightly. "My father wanted to take a second wife," he confessed.

"So they divorced?"

"Eventually."

"What does that mean?" Jemma asked, turning onto her side.

"It means it took her nearly five years to successfully divorce him. My father didn't want the divorce, so he contested it."

"He loved her," Jemma said.

"I don't think he loved her. But he didn't want her to shame him. He was the king. How could his wife leave him?"

Jemma was silent a long moment. "Your mother loved him. She didn't want to share him?"

"I don't remember love. I remember fighting. Years of fighting." And crying. Years of crying. But not the tears of Saidia women. His mother only cried quietly, late at night, when she thought no one was listening.

But he had listened. He had heard her weeping. And he had never done anything about it.

Jemma put her hand on his chest, her palm warm against his skin. "She had to know when she married your father that he might take another wife."

"She said he promised her that he would never take another wife. She said he had it added to their wedding contract. But it wasn't there. My father said my mother never added a clause, and that she knew all along there would be other wives. That she was only the first." He hesitated, trying not to remember too much of those years, and how awful it'd been with the endless fighting, and then his mother crying late at night when the servants were asleep. "By the time the divorce was final, he'd taken three more wives."

Mikael looked away from the sympathy in Jemma's eyes,

uncomfortable with it. He focused on the ceiling of the pavilion, and the whirring of the fan blades. "I was eleven when
the divorce was finalized."

Her fingers curled against his chest. "Did you go live with
her?"

"No. I stayed with my father."

"You wanted to?"

"I didn't have a choice. I had to stay with my father." He
glanced at her. "In Saidia, like many Arab countries, mothers
do not retain custody of the children in a divorce. The children usually go to the father, or the closest male relative, and
the sons always remain with the father."

She rolled closer to him, both hands against his chest now.
"But you saw your mom sometimes?"

"No."

"Never?"

"She was expelled from Saidia." He reached out and caught
her hair again, playing with the strand. "I wouldn't see her
again for almost twenty years. In fact not until just a few
months before your sister Morgan's wedding."

"What?"

He let go of the strand. "I couldn't see her after she left, and
then, I wouldn't see her."

Jemma just stared at him, eyes wide, her expression
shocked. "You punished her for the divorce."

He shrugged. "I had a hard time forgiving her for divorcing
my father. Because yes, she knew that by divorcing my father,
she'd lose me. He made it clear he wouldn't let me leave with
her. But she divorced him anyway. She chose to leave Saidia
and leave me behind." Mikael abruptly pulled away, rolling
from the low cushions to stand up, and offered her his hand.
"It's hot. We talked. I think it's time to cool off with a swim."

They swam and splashed for a half hour until their lunch was
brought to them. They sat in their wet swimsuits beneath the
shade of a palm tree eating lunch.

As Jemma nibbled on her salad she watched Mikael from beneath her lashes.

She was still processing everything he'd told her in the pavilion about his parents' marriage and divorce. Knowing that his mother was an American made it worse as Jemma found it so easy to identify with the woman, and how she must have felt in this Arab country with her powerful royal husband. And yet, even though his mother was an American and unhappy here, how could she leave her child behind?

How could she adore her son but then walk away from him?

"Do you look like your father?" she asked Mikael as they finished their meal.

Mikael ran his hand through his short black hair. "I wish I hadn't told you about the divorce."

"Why?"

"I'm not comfortable with it. Or proud of my father. Or myself. Or of any of the decisions made."

Jemma understood, more than he knew. She'd wanted to go live with her mother when her parents divorced, but she hadn't wanted to lose her father. And for years after the divorce, she'd still looked forward to seeing him, and she'd cherished the gifts he'd sent in the early years after the divorce—the dolls, the pretty clothes, the hot pink bike for her twelfth birthday—but then her parents quarreled again when she was thirteen, and all contact stopped. Her father disappeared from her life completely.

She hated him, and yet she loved him. She missed him and needed him. She went to London to start over, to get away from her past and herself, and she thought she had. Until the news broke that he'd stolen hundreds of millions of dollars of his clients' money.

Jemma looked at Mikael. "I sometimes think that if my parents hadn't divorced, and my father had been more involved in our lives, he would have made different choices. I think that if maybe we'd stayed close, he would have realized how much we loved him and needed him."

Mikael's expression was incredulous. "You blame yourself?"

"I try to understand what happened."

"He was selfish."

She flinched. "You're right."

"He was the worst sort of man because he pretended to care, pretended to understand what vulnerable people needed, and then he destroyed them."

Jemma closed her eyes.

"Who befriends older women and then robs them?" he demanded.

Eyes closed, she shook her head.

"Your father told my mother to refinance her house and give him the money to invest, promising her amazing returns, but didn't invest any of it. He just put it into his own account. He drained her account for himself." Mikael's voice vibrated with contempt and fury. "It disgusts me." He drew a rough breath. "We should not talk about this."

She nodded, sick, flattened.

Silence stretched, heavy and suffocating.

Mikael left his chair and paced the length of the pool. Jemma's eyes burned and she had to work very hard not to cry.

She was so ashamed. She felt raw and exposed. In the Arab world, she represented her family. She was an extension of her family, an extension of her father. Here in Saidia his shame attached to her. His shame would always taint her.

Silently Jemma left the pool, returning to the Chamber of Innocence to shower in the white marble bath, and shampoo her hair to wash the chlorine out. As she worked the suds in, she gritted her teeth, holding all the emotion in.

She wasn't sad. She wasn't scared. She wasn't lonely. She wasn't miserable in any way.

No, miserable would be living in Connecticut, trying to find a place to stay, wondering who might take her in, if maybe one of her mother's few remaining friends might allow her to crash on a couch or in a guest bedroom.

Rinsing her hair, she lifted her face to the spray. It was so hard to believe that her family had once had everything. Hard to believe they'd been placed on a pedestal. Their beautiful, lavish lifestyle had been envied and much discussed. Magazines featured their Caribbean home, their sprawling shingle house in Connecticut, the log cabin in Sun Valley. They had money for trips, money for clothes, money for dinners out.

Jemma turned the shower off, wrung the excess water from her hair wondering if any of it had been real.

Had any of it been their money to spend?

How long had her father taken advantage of his clients?

Bundled in a towel, she left the bathroom, crawled into the white and silver bed and pulled the soft Egyptian sheet all the way over her, to the top of her head.

It was hard being a Copeland. Hard living with so much shame. Work had been the only thing that kept her going, especially after Damien walked away from her. Work gave her something to do, something to think about. Working allowed her—even if briefly—to be someone else.

Now she just needed to get home and back to work. Work was still the answer. She simply had to get through these next seven days. And seven nights.

Jemma drew a big breath for courage, aware that the night would soon be here.

CHAPTER TEN

SHE WAS TO dress for dinner.

That's what the card attached to the garment bag instructed: *Dress for dinner. I will collect you at nine.*

Jemma unzipped the bag, and pushed away tissue to discover a sumptuous silk gown the color of ripe peaches. Ornate gold beading wrapped the hem and the long sleeve of the asymmetrical gown. The gown gathered over one shoulder creating a full flowing sleeve, while leaving the other shoulder and arm bare.

It was beautiful. Exotic. A dress for a desert princess.

There was a jewelry box in the bottom of the garment bag containing gold chandelier earrings studded with diamonds and pearls. They looked old, and very valuable.

She lifted an earring, holding it to her ear and looked in the mirror. The delicate gold and diamond earring was stunning against her dark loose hair. She'd wear her hair down tonight, dress like a desert princess. She hoped Mikael would not be angry this evening. The morning had been fun. He'd been a great companion. For a couple hours she'd forgotten why she was here.

He arrived at her door promptly at nine. Jemma had been ready for almost an hour. Opening the door she discovered he was dressed in his traditional robe again and she felt a stab of disappointment, preferring him in Western clothes. She felt more comfortable when he looked familiar, and not like the foreign sheikh he was.

"You look stunning," he said.

She smiled, hiding her nervousness. "Thank you."

"Do you know what we are doing for dinner?" he asked, leading her from the room, and down the outer corridor.

"No."

He smiled down at her. "Good."

He escorted her all the way to the front of the Kasbah, and out through the grand wooden doors. A car and driver waited for them.

The driver opened the back door of the black sedan. Jemma glanced at Mikael before climbing in. But he said nothing and his expression gave nothing away.

With Mikael seated next to her, the driver left the walled Kasbah. Soon they were driving through the desert, the car flying down the ribbon of asphalt. Moonlight bathed the miles of undulating sand.

Mikael pointed to the landscape beyond the tinted window. "This, my queen, is all yours."

She looked out the window, at the vast desert, and then back at Mikael, struggling to keep a straight face. "It is truly lovely sand."

"Are you making fun of my desert?"

"Absolutely not."

"Good." His eyes gleamed. "Because I value every single grain in this desert."

She smiled, and he smiled back and then his smile faded. He reached out and lightly touched the ornate gold chandelier dangling from her lobe. "These look beautiful on you."

"They are exquisite," she agreed.

"But you said you do not value jewels."

She looked at him warily. "Not as much as some women, no."

"But you value...*talking*."

He sounded so pained that her lips curved and her heart turned over. "Sharing," she explained.

"How do you feel about apologies?"

She lifted her brows. "In my experience, women love them. Men tend to hate them."

He smiled faintly. "That seems true in my experience as well." He hesitated. "And as difficult as it is for me to say I'm sorry, I owe you an apology. I was curt with you earlier, at the pool, and I focused my anger on you, when it's your father I am angry with."

She shifted uncomfortably. "You don't have to apologize. Every word you said was true. Your mother was treated terribly—"

"Yes," he interrupted quietly. "But that doesn't excuse how I spoke to you. And it doesn't make my behavior acceptable. You were reaching out to me, and sharing your experiences, and your feelings, and I lashed out, hurtfully. I am sorry for that. I take no pride in my faults, and as you have seen, I've many."

For a long moment Jemma could think of nothing to say. It was hard to speak when her eyes burned and her throat ached. She was surprised, and touched, by his honesty, never mind the humility. "Of course I forgive you. We all have things that hurt us."

His dark head inclined. "I am sensitive with regards to my mother, because my father mistreated her, and then I mistreated her, too."

"You were just a boy at the time of their divorce."

His features tightened. "I hated her for getting the divorce." The words were said bluntly, sharply. "Was her pride so important? Was her pride more important than me? She knew when the divorce was finalized, she'd leave the country, without me." He extended his legs as much as he could. "I'd be lying if I said that I understand now. Because I don't. Maybe I won't ever. But it was terrible then, being eleven, and knowing my mother chose to leave me."

Jemma reached to him, put her hand on his arm. "Perhaps she didn't think she'd really lose you. Maybe she thought things would turn out differently."

"How?"

"Maybe she thought your father would back down, change his mind, not move forward and marry a second wife. Or maybe she had worked out some sort of alternative custody arrangement. Maybe your father had agreed to share you...or even grant her custody while you were a child." Jemma leaned toward him, the delicate gold and diamond earring tinkling. "If your father had deceived her about the marriage contract, who knows what he might have said to her? Or promised her?"

He glanced at her. "But I didn't know that as a boy. I didn't know he was to blame. That he was the one who'd lied. So I blamed her."

"You were angry with her."

"I hated her."

"And then as an adult you learned the truth."

"Yes." His lips curved but the smile didn't reach his eyes. "And I hated him."

"You told him that?"

"No, not then."

"But you did go to your mother? You tried to make amends?"

He sat still, expression blank. "I waited a long time. I waited too long. If I'd gone to her earlier, and tried to help her earlier, she might not have relied so much on others. On outsiders."

"Like my father."

He nodded. "I should have been there for her sooner." His expression turned mocking. "You can see why I don't like talking about the past. I was not a good person. I was a very destructive person, and that is why I'm so driven to redeem the Karims and restore honor to our family and Saidia. I cannot let my mother's death be in vain."

"I think you judge yourself too harshly," she said gently.

"Power is never to be abused."

"I have yet to see you abuse your power. If anything, you appear determined to be fair, even if your idea of justice is very different from how we, in the West, would view it."

"Then perhaps I have begun to make amends." He smiled at

her, but his smile failed to light his dark eyes, then he glanced out the window, and nodded. "See those lights in the distance? That's where we are having dinner tonight, my queen."

Jemma gazed out at the swathe of darkness with the pin-pricks of light. "Is that a restaurant?"

"No." Amusement warmed his voice. "Not a restaurant. At least not the way you'd think of it. But it is where we're eating."

CHAPTER ELEVEN

JEMMA WAS SPEECHLESS as Mikael escorted her into the tent. Plush crimson carpets covered the sand. Rustic copper lanterns hung from the tent's wooden poles. More lanterns and candles glowed on low tables. From the fire pit outside the tent she caught a whiff of roasted lamb. As if on cue, her stomach growled.

Mikael looked at her. "Ready to eat?"

"Starving," she admitted.

"You're in luck. Our first course is ready."

The grilled vegetables and meat were served with a couscous flavored with slivered almonds and currants. They scooped up the couscous and meat with chunks of warm sesame bread and Mikael was fascinating company, as always.

Jemma welcomed his stories about Saidia's history and tribal lore, understanding now why he'd worn his robes tonight. This was his desert. His world.

Just then the evening breeze played with the sheer silk panels lining the tent, parting the material, giving her a glimpse of the white moon and the deep purple black sky.

The night sky was so bright and the stars dazzled. The sky never looked like this in London or New York. But in the vastness of the desert, with darkness stretching in every direction, the sky literally glowed with light.

"Beautiful night," Mikael said, following her gaze.

She nodded. "Amazing. I feel like I'm in a fairy tale."

He hesitated a moment. "I think after the honeymoon, we

should go visit your mother. I don't want her to worry about you. She has enough worries already."

"You'd let me travel with you?"

"With me, and without me. Marriage isn't a prison, and I'd never keep you from your family, or opportunities, provided you were able to fulfill your duties as my wife and queen." He paused, studying her. "I have a house in London. It's large, and comfortable. Well located. It needs you. Someone to fill it with people and parties."

Jemma looked away, emotion making her chest ache. "Now you're just teasing me. Tempting me with possibilities that are...impossible."

"How so?"

"You shouldn't dangle things before me. Or opportunities. I'm strong, but not that strong. If I stayed here, it shouldn't be for things." She turned to look at him again, her gaze locking with his. "It should be for the right reasons. It should be for you."

For a moment there was just silence. And then Mikael leaned forward, captured her face in his hands and kissed her lightly on the lips before releasing her.

Jemma's heart turned over. Her lips tingled. She nearly pressed her fingers to her mouth to stop the throbbing.

"Next time I see Sheikh Azizzi I must thank him," Mikael said, his deep voice pitched even lower. "I was angry with him in Haslam. I was angry that he'd try to saddle me with you, but obviously he knew something I didn't."

"Saddle doesn't sound very complimentary."

"You weren't happy about it, either."

No, that was true. She was shocked, angry, desperate. But happy? No.

But she almost felt happy right now. For the first time in months and months she felt calm. She felt content. She felt as if she could breathe.

Which is why she had to be careful. She needed to keep her guard up. It was vital she not let Mikael get too much closer.

While they'd talked a servant had removed the dishes, re-placing the platters and bowls with trays of delicate biscuits and dried fruits.

"You really like London?" Mikael asked her, taking one of the dates stuffed with cheese and rolling it between his fin-gers. "It was never a culture shock?"

"I liked it from the start. No one paid me any attention. I felt free there." She selected one of the flaky almond cookies and broke it in half. "It's different now. I'm known, and more alone than ever."

"You're lonely?"

She nodded. "Yes. I miss what I had. Not the things, but the friends, the activities, the energy. I used to wake up every day, excited to see what the day would bring. Now I just get by. Push through."

"Once we return to Ketama, once everyone knows of our marriage, you will discover that doors presently closed to you, will open. As my wife, you will be welcome everywhere. As my wife, no one would dare to shame you, or exclude you."

Jemma popped half the cookie in her mouth and chewed, but her mouth had gone dry, and the cookie tasted like saw-dust. "I don't want to be accepted because people are afraid of alienating you. I want to be accepted because people like me." Her eyes suddenly burned and she took a sip from her golden goblet. "It hurts to be scorned."

"Which is why you need my protection. I do not want you to suffer more than you have."

His gaze met hers and held. His dark eyes burned into her. She felt her pulse quicken, and butterflies flit wildly in her middle, her body humming with awareness.

Mikael would be a protective husband. He would probably be generous to a fault. He'd already showered her with gifts and trinkets, and was good at paying her compliments.

She wondered what marriage to him would be like. Not the honeymoon part, but the *ever after* part.

What kind of husband would he be?

Would he have expectations for his wife's behavior? Rules for the relationship? What would he not permit, or tolerate?

Mikael's eyes met hers, and held. "You have something on your mind."

"You can read me too easily. Have you always been so attentive to women?"

"No. Never." He leaned over and refilled her goblet. "I'm usually accused of being insensitive and self-absorbed."

"Are you different with me?"

"It would seem so."

"Because I am your wife?"

"Because I can't help but pay you attention. You command it."

"I *command* it. Interesting."

"You are a queen now. You are in a position of significance."

"Careful. The power might go to my head." But she was laughing as she said it, and from his lazy smile, she knew he was amused. "Do you enjoy your power?"

He thought about the question for a moment and then nodded. "Sheikhs are allowed to be as demanding as they like. It is the benefit of being royal. But power carries responsibility to provide for one's family, and people, and protect them as well. This is where my father failed. This is where I cannot fail."

"I do not think you will. You have the right mindset. You are focused on the right goals."

"I am less focused now that you are here," he admitted. "With you here I find I only want to think about you."

"It is your honeymoon."

"*Our* honeymoon," he corrected, reaching out to stroke her cheek, and then press his thumb to her lips.

Heat raced through her, followed by a frisson of sensation that made her breasts tingle and her legs quiver. She felt so aware of him and the awareness was a bittersweet tension, her body humming in response. She ached inside, at the place where her thighs joined, and she hated wanting…needing…

Jemma squeezed her thighs together, denying the need, and

struggling to ignore the way her skin tingled, sending fresh darts of sensation from her breasts to her belly.

His gaze met hers and held, and he couldn't know what she was thinking or feeling, but she blushed anyway, heat racing through her, making her hot and cold.

She was attracted to him. She was responding to him. It crossed her mind that she just might be in over her head.

"Yes, *laeela*?" he asked, reclining against the cushions. "What are you thinking?"

She shouldn't have agreed to this. She shouldn't have played this game. It was a game she could lose. "You…your government," she stuttered, thinking she could never admit that sex was on her brain. Sex, seduction, sensual lovemaking…no, better to keep the conversation away from the personal.

"Our government?" he repeated, eyes crinkling. "Politics intrigue you?"

No, but you intrigue me. You make me wonder about everything I do not yet know. Instead she crossed her legs and tried to calm herself. "Did you inherit your power?"

"Yes."

"Because you were first born, of the first wife?"

"Yes."

"Do you have brothers and sisters?"

"Yes. Many."

Interesting. "Are any of them in a government position?"

"There are three that have inherited significant tribal power and wealth, but so far these half brothers prefer to avoid work and responsibility."

"They are the sons of your father's second wife?"

"She had three boys in quick succession. They are handsome, popular, and quite headstrong."

"You like them?"

"I love them." He hesitated, smiling wryly. "And I imagine I will like them even better once they begin to grow up."

She grimaced. "It's easy to be self-indulgent when you're given everything. I grew up in a wealthy family, surrounded by peers from equally wealthy families. It's not the real world. As difficult as it's been this past year, I'm glad to be living in the real world. I know now who my true friends are. I know what matters."

"I hope one day my brothers discover what's true, and real."

"Perhaps they need an incentive to mature. Perhaps it's too easy for them…being young, handsome, and wealthy."

"They do have it too easy. Nothing is worse than a spoiled, billionaire prince."

"Were you ever like that? A spoiled, billionaire prince?"

"It was different for me. I've always known I would be king. And I've always been conscious that I was the son from the bad first wife, the American wife. I've tried hard to do the right thing, to avoid additional scrutiny and criticism."

She studied him, still warm, still so fascinated by this man and how he made her feel things and want things. But she had to be careful. She needed to remain in control. "We don't hear much about Saidia in the news in the US."

"That's because we try to stay out of the news, and we are a stable country. Historically, the Karims have gone to great lengths to ensure our people's happiness."

"So people are happy?"

"Yes. We have excellent schools and health care. Girls are actively encouraged to attend school, even pursue higher education. Marriage is forbidden under the age of eighteen, without parental consent." His dark eyes glowed. "Does that answer all of your questions? Or is there something else you'd like to know?"

The gleam in his eye was dangerous. It made her pulse leap, and her stomach lurch. Just like that, she felt him…near her, around her, as if they were connected. One. Which was ludicrous. She barely knew him and they weren't touching. He was reclining four or five feet away.

And yet her skin tingled and her insides felt strange, her nerve endings wound too tightly.

The desert wasn't safe. Not with Mikael in it.

"And what are you thinking of now?" he asked, his deep voice pitched low, making her think of dark sensual things that she shouldn't be thinking, not when alone with him.

"What is your seduction plan?" she asked. "What's supposed to happen tonight?"

He didn't smile, but she could have sworn he was laughing at her.

"What do you think is going to happen?"

She hated it when he answered her question with another question. "No idea. That's why I asked."

"I have an idea of how I think the evening will go," he said, watching her with that lazy interest, which she knew now wasn't lazy at all.

He was paying close attention to her, listening attentively to everything she said, observing everything she did.

He, too, was aware of the energy between them. Something was happening. She felt the heat and tension, the prickling awareness. It was sexual. And tangible. Her gown which had been so comfortable earlier now felt hot and tight, constricting.

"You are impossible," she whispered, breathless. He made her breathless.

Did he know the effect he had on her? Did he know that he made her curious? Weak?

She felt weak now, and hot, so hot, as tiny tongues of desire made her nipples tighten inside the delicate fabric of her dress.

"Yesterday was touch," he said. "I gave you a massage."

"Yes," she agreed. "It was an incredible massage, too."

"Today...what have we done so far?"

"Kissed," she whispered.

"Exactly. Today I can only kiss you."

"Oh." She tried to stifle the stab of disappointment.

"Fortunately, there are many different ways I can kiss you."

He stood up and walked around the perimeter of the tent, dropping the heavy panels, making the soft sheer silk curtains flutter in as the outside covers fell. "Different places I can kiss you."

Jemma held her breath as he continued to walk around the tent, closing them off from the night, and his staff, tying the cords on the inner panels, sealing them into a private world.

Soon the tent was a cocoon, and darker, with the loss of moonlight.

Mikael reached for a lantern and moved it, hanging it a little behind her. "Different places you might want me to kiss you." He moved another lamp, bringing it closer to the table next to her. "The lamps are so I can see you," he said. "I want to see you."

Her insides wobbled. She bit down on the inside of her lip to hide her flurry of nerves.

"I want to see you as I make you come," he added.

Her lips parted, shocked. She sat up taller, her hands going to her knees.

She shouldn't like it when he talked to her like this, but she did. He was untamed. "You think I'm joking?" he asked.

She didn't know how to answer, wasn't sure what to do or say, so she simply looked at him, chewing on the inside of her lip, nervous. Anxious. Excited.

This was his night. His game. He held the power.

"I have waited all afternoon for this," he said, prowling around her again, dark eyes burning, emphasizing the high hard lines of his cheekbones, jaw and chin. "Waited to see you naked. Waited to taste your skin."

A funny pang pinched her heart. She struggled to breathe.

He was frightening, arrogant, headstrong.

He was also overwhelmingly powerful, physical, and sexual.

She'd never met another man like him and she shouldn't be drawn to him, but she was.

For some reason she responded to him, to his edges and complexity. She was intrigued by his harsh justice, as well as his sensual nature.

She craved the sensual side of him. She wanted the sensation and pleasure of being bedded by him. She wanted to sleep with him. Wanted him naked against her, wanted his bare hands on her breasts and his mouth on her body. Wanted to be pinned beneath him and feel him thrust hard and deep, burying his body inside hers.

He moved in front of her, crouching before her, and tilted her chin up to look into her eyes. "I want you," he said, his deep voice velvety soft. "But I want your pleasure more."

And then he kissed her, deeply, the kiss so slow and so erotic that it immediately torched her senses, making her head spin.

He pressed her back against the soft carpet, and stretched out over her. She could still feel the press of his arousal through his robes. He was long and thick and hard.

His hand found her breast through her thin gown, his fingers rubbing and pinching and kneading her taut nipple. She trembled and sighed as he focused on one breast, and then the other.

She was hot and wet and aching for more.

Jemma pressed her thighs together, craving satisfaction.

"Don't come," he murmured against her mouth. "Relax. Let me enjoy your beautiful body."

"You're turning me on," she answered.

He shifted his weight, his hips grinding against hers.

The head of his arousal pressed against her pubic bone. His warmth made her want to open to him. She wanted him inside her, not on her. "This is torture," she whispered.

"Good torture," he said, drawing away, and placing a kiss on her chin, and then her neck, and he kissed his way down to her breastbone, and then lower, over the fabric of her gown covering her belly and then lower still, kissing the V of her thighs, his breath heating her skin, making the silk gown warm and damp. Making her warmer, damper.

She groaned as his teeth lightly nipped her. "Please," she whispered. "Be nice."

"I'm being very nice," he said.

And then he shifted his weight off her completely, and he reached for the hem of her gown.

Her heart slammed into her rib cage as he pushed her skirt

up, and carefully tugged her lace panties down, sliding them off her ankles, over each of her jeweled shoes. Then he parted her thighs, pushing them wide, and settled between them to kiss the inside of her knee, and then continued kissing her inner thigh, slowly working his way to her most intimate place.

Jemma gasped as his warm mouth settled on her, his tongue sliding up and down, stroking her.

She shuddered with pleasure, overwhelmed by the intense sensation. His mouth and touch made her feel so many different and disorienting emotions and sensations, filling her head with pictures and colors, all intense and vivid, electric and erotic.

The eroticism exposed her. The eroticism challenged her.

Who was she? What was she? What was true?

Jemma cried out as his tongue pushed deeper, his mouth cool where she felt so warm, his tongue circling provocatively across her taut, sensitive nub. At the sound of her cry, his hands pushed her thighs wider, his thumbs pressing against her bottom, holding her open.

It was shocking. Shocking because it was *him*, doing this to *her*.

She'd been raised to think for herself, raised to be independent, successful, and her brain told her she shouldn't enjoy this…being handled, managed, seduced. But her body liked it, and she was beginning to realize there was another side of her, a side she found rather frightening.

It was darkly sensual, and wanton. Illicit, too.

It was almost like an erotic dream…sexy, and sensual, and intense…

So intense, especially when he sucked and there was no holding back. The tension and pressure grew, electric sensation shooting through her. She couldn't resist it, couldn't resist him. With a cry she climaxed, shattering from his expert tongue and the intimate kiss.

For a moment after, Jemma didn't know who she was, or where she was. For a moment, she was just part of the night and the diamond studded sky. She felt endless, and open and free.

And then little by little she returned to herself, and him.

Opening her eyes, she looked at him, unsure as to what his reaction would be.

His dark eyes were hooded, his expression watchful. But protective. Maybe even a little possessive.

"Say something," she whispered.

"You're beautiful."

Her cheeks burned. "I don't even know how…or why…." She licked her upper lip, her mouth dry, her heart hammering. "Or what happened."

"I do." He crouched next to her, lifting a strand of hair from her warm, flushed face. "I wanted you to feel good. Did I make you feel good?"

"Yes."

"Then I feel good."

CHAPTER TWELVE

AN HOUR AND a half later, back at the Kasbah, Jemma lay in the center of the enormous bronze jeweled bed in the Topaz Chamber, and watched the blades of the fan turn overhead, hearing but not listening to the hum of the fan, seeing the orange silk panels at the window stir. The cool air felt good against her heated skin.

The soft whir of the fan's blades and the caress of cool air soothed her.

She was panicking. But there was no need to panic. Everything would be okay. Nothing terrible had happened, nothing life changing. He'd kissed her. Touched her. Brought her to an orgasm. It wasn't the end of the world, and it was not as if she hadn't ever indulged in oral sex before. Damien hadn't loved to do it, but that didn't mean she couldn't enjoy it.

And yet it was all so confusing. Her feelings. Her desire. And that rush of guilty pleasure, after he'd brought her to a climax.

Why had she felt guilty? Why should she feel bad for feeling pleasure? Was it because his lovemaking lacked love? Was it because his lovemaking had been so erotic?

She wished she knew. She wished she understood. She wished she wasn't alone now, in the bed, feeling this way.

Mikael had said he'd return soon. He'd told her after he escorted her back to the chamber, that he needed to make a phone call, and promised to come back as soon as he could, but it'd been an hour. She was still waiting.

"What's wrong?" Mikael's voice sounded in the doorway.

She sat up quickly, startled, and yet also relieved.

"You're back," she said, drawing the sheet closer to her breasts. She'd changed from the evening gown into the peach satin nightgown with the gold straps that had been left out for her.

"Yes. Disappointed?" he drawled.

"No. I'm glad."

"Are you?"

She nodded, feeling strangely undone. Her throat ached. She swallowed around the lump. "I…missed…you."

He turned on a small golden lantern in the corner; the soft light illuminated the wide gold and orange stripes on the walls, this room as exotic as the tent earlier in the desert.

He'd showered and changed into black silk pajama pants and a black robe that he'd left open over his bare chest. His skin gleamed, gold. "I was gone longer than I intended," he said, reaching into the pocket of his robe. "But I've come bearing gifts."

"You know how I feel about presents," she said, as he took a seat next to her on the bed.

"Yes, but you should know by now how much I like giving them." He drew a wide jeweled gold cuff from the pocket of the robe, the thick cuff inlaid with pink diamonds, rubies, and topaz and fastened the bangle around her wrist

She glanced down at the heavy gold bangle, thickly studded with jewels. It had to be worth hundreds of thousands of dollars. "Are these all real gems?"

"Yes."

"It's old."

"At least one hundred and fifty years."

The ornate bracelet on her wrist slid forward, exquisite pink and ruby stones catching the light, casting prisms on the wall. A jeweled bed. A jeweled wrist. But jewels wouldn't keep her here. Jewels sparkled but they couldn't keep her warm. They wouldn't make her feel needed, loved. And that was what she wanted most. Love.

"Thank you," she said, giving her hand another light shake, admiring the enormous stones in the thick gold, using the time to divert his attention so he wouldn't see the tears in her eyes.

Things were becoming more complicated. She'd begun to feel things and if she wasn't careful, she'd make a mistake. A terrible mistake. And enough mistakes had been made.

"My pleasure," he answered.

She glanced up at him, hoping he wouldn't see her chaotic emotions. "Did you just return to give me this?"

"No." He took off his robe, and tossed it onto a low chair in the corner. "I forgot something."

"You did?"

"Yes. You." He went to the gold lantern and turned off the light before returning to the bed. "Scoot over. And don't worry. You can relax. You are safe. Nothing is happening tonight. I just want to sleep near my beautiful wife."

In bed, he drew her close to him, his arm loose around her waist, his hand resting on her hip.

For a moment she couldn't breathe. For a moment she waited, wondering if panic would hit. If she'd become nervous or uncomfortable.

If she'd dislike being held by him, held close to him.

None of those things happened.

He felt good. He felt warm. She felt safe.

Jemma woke up alone.

She told herself she didn't mind. Told herself she was glad. She needed space. She liked her independence. But it'd felt good having Mikael near her last night. She'd slept deeply for a change and she woke rested, and anxious to see him.

But Mikael didn't put in an appearance that morning. Instead there was a purple bikini and delicate violet silk cover-up waiting for her, along with a note telling her that tonight she'd sleep in the Amethyst Chamber.

Jemma changed into the pretty purple bikini and slipped the delicate silk cover up over her head, letting the light fabric settle against her tummy and thighs.

Purple was a good color for her. It flattered her skin. She wondered if Mikael would have a gift made from amethyst gems for her tonight. A necklace, a ring, or possibly earrings. She didn't want it, or need it, but it gave her something to think about, rather than her emotions.

She missed Mikael.

She didn't want to be alone.

But she had breakfast outside and then paced the courtyard, swimming when she grew too hot.

Lunch came and went, with her again eating by herself inside one of the air conditioned pavilions, needing the shade.

It was a long day waiting. She grew restless and angry. She peeled off the filmy violet cover up and swam again, and then stretched facedown on a lounge chair, the high desert temperature drying her purple suit almost instantly.

She buried her face in the crook of her arm, telling herself to relax, and calm down. She was getting herself worked up over nothing. Mikael would join her when he could. He'd be there as soon as he could manage it. There was no reason to feel so desperate, or lonely…

And then he was there.

Just like that.

His shadow stretched over her lounge chair, blocking the sun, and she turned over onto her back and looked up at him.

He gazed down at her with dark, smoky eyes. He was dressed in his robes. She suspected he'd had business earlier. But she didn't ask and he didn't tell her.

She raised a hand to shield her eyes and she let her gaze wander over him, up over his chest, to his neck, his hard jaw, the chiseled cheek and then to his eyes. He had ridiculously beautiful eyes. She'd kill for his lashes. It would save her a fortune in eyeliner and mascara.

"You smile." Mikael's deep husky voice vibrated between them, coloring the air, filling the space around them.

Heat danced through her, little sparklers lighting nerve endings beneath her skin. She flexed her feet, feeling her toes curl.

Amazing how little it took for him to turn her on.

Just a long glance from his dark eyes.

A word from his lips.

A certain pitch in his voice.

That's all it took and everything within her melted, wanting. Wanting him and what he did to her, and what he could make her feel.

Jemma drew a slow breath, and then exhaled just as slowly, trying to calm the frantic beating of her heart. "You have the longest, darkest eyelashes," she said, hating the slightly breathless note in her voice, knowing he'd notice. He always did. "I should steal them. You don't need them. I'm the model, not you."

The edge of his mouth lifted. He sat down on the edge of her lounge chair, his hand settling on her knees and then sliding up a couple inches on her thigh. "No Saidian queen has ever held a job."

"Are you saying I can't work if I am your queen?"

"You *are* my queen, and I haven't made any decisions with regard to your career. Although truthfully, it would be very unusual in Saidia, and would probably create a great deal of controversy, if you did continue working."

"So we know what that means."

He tapped the tip of her nose. "We don't know what that means, Miss Smarty Pants." He moved his hand to her thigh, his palm warm against her skin. "Would you miss modeling?"

"I would miss working."

"But not modeling specifically?"

She shrugged, and struggled to focus, which wasn't easy with the warmth of his hand stealing into her thigh. "I enjoyed my job until recently…when everyone dropped me."

"Could you be happy doing other things?"

He'd begun to draw invisible circles on her thigh, setting the nerve endings on fire.

"Such as?" she asked, her voice growing husky.

"Making public appearances. Talking to girls and advocating literacy. Making love to me. Having babies."

Every word he spoke was accompanied by another swoop of his finger across her bare skin, flaming the nerve endings all the while moving closer to her tiny purple bikini bottoms.

She was tempted to press her knees together to stop his fingers and yet she loved his touch, wanted more, wanted him to strip the bottoms off of her and part her thighs and settle between them again, and put his mouth on her, using his tongue and fingers to trace the shape of her soft folds and the tight sensitive clit—

"You're distracted," Mikael said, leaning in to kiss her, even as his palm slid over her thigh to her hip.

She shivered at the caress and the brush of his lips over hers. He pushed her heavy damp hair from her face and kissed her again, more deeply.

She sighed, as he lifted his head. She wanted more, not less. "Maybe a little," she agreed. "Where have you been?"

"I had some business to attend to."

"Out here?" she asked glancing around. "In the middle of the desert?"

"There is technology." He dipped his head, kissed her again, another tingling, soul-stirring kiss that made shivers race through her.

She reached up to touch his face. "When can I use your technology?"

"When the honeymoon is over."

"Is this tradition, or your rule?"

"Both. I want you to myself, and tradition says I have eight days to do just that…keep you hidden from the world during my attempt to win your heart."

"Are you trying to win my heart?" she asked, as his hand

stroked up her waist to brush the curve of her breast. "Or win my body?"

"I think I've already done that."

"You sound so sure of yourself," she said, gasping as his hand slipped beneath the fabric of her bikini top to cup her breast.

"I am." His head dropped and he kissed her again, even as he kneaded her breast and teased her sensitive nipple.

Desire surged through her, a hot, insatiable current that scalded her skin and made her melt on the inside. She leaned into his hand, her body aching, straining for more contact.

"You're starting it again," she whispered against his mouth. "You're wreaking havoc on my defenses."

His dark gaze held hers, the irises dark, mysterious. "You don't need defenses against me."

"Oh, I absolutely do. If I lose control, all bets are off."

"If you lose control, you're still safe with me." He kissed her again, and then caressed her lower lip, and the hollow beneath. "You will always be safe with me."

"I don't know, because this feels pretty dangerous."

He smiled a wicked smile which made her breath catch and her pulse race, making her heart pound and hum with the rest of her body.

His dark gaze settled on her mouth, and the quiver of her lower lip. "Good. Because this is desire."

The quiver of her lip intensified, along with the reckless rhythm of her heart. Blood drummed through her veins, warming her, making her skin hot and sensitive.

"And desire is important," he added, drawing his fingertip from her lower lip, down the middle of her chin, and lower still, down her neck to the base of her throat, and then on to her breastbone. It was such a light stroke, but slow, and long, and he lit every nerve ending he touched. "Desire makes us feel alive."

"It's so sexual."

"Mmm," he murmured, the corner of his mouth curving, and yet it wasn't a smile. It looked like hunger. "Is that a problem?"

She shivered, and would have looked away if he hadn't caught her chin, and forced her gaze to meet his. Her mouth dried. She licked her lips, blood roaring in her ears. "Sex without emotion is empty," she said.

"Is it? Even when you have this intense chemistry?" he asked, stroking the curve of her breasts, avoiding the taut, straining nipple. "How can this be empty?"

Her thoughts slowed, became tangled, her senses taking over, smothering reason. Was this empty? Was this connection bad?

Mikael's fingertip drew slow, lazy circles down the slope of her breast to the valley between, and then down across her flat belly to gently press against her through the material of her bikini bottoms.

She sighed as her head lit up with color and lights and pleasure.

"We enjoy each other," he added, tracing her softness, his knuckle brushing against her where she was so very sensitive. "We've been affectionate. We both feel a strong physical connection. What is missing?"

Love.

She wanted more than sex, more than pleasure. She wanted love. But it was so hard to say when he was touching her so intimately, making her head spin, and her senses pop and explode.

It was hard to focus, even harder for her to speak. "A relationship can't just be about sex," she said. "And I want more than pleasure."

"You don't think pleasure can lead to more?" His fingers slipped beneath the material to caress her intimately. She was hot and slick and he teased her, making her gasp and squeeze her thighs together to ignore what was happening inside of her.

"Can't pleasure generate love?" he persisted, before leaning over her and kissing one taut nipple through her top.

"I don't…think…so," she said, sucking in a breath as he

sucked her, drawing on her hard enough to create sharp pinches of sensation, the pleasure so intense it was almost like pain.

As he worked her breast he pressed his fingers into her, stroking her deep and rhythmically, matching the draw on her nipple.

Fire streaked from her breast to her womb. She felt her inner muscles clench him, her body already so hot and wet she knew she wouldn't last, knew she couldn't hold back. He had magic in his hands, and he knew just how to touch her, just how to seduce her. He could make her his slave with just a kiss and a touch...

"But you don't know for sure," he said, stroking deep, creating a maddening friction. His dark eyes sparked. "Pleasure happens in the mind. Love happens there, too." He leaned close, his lips grazing hers. "Why can't one lead to the other?"

She leaned in to the kiss, kissing him with desperation and hunger, as the tease of desire became a fierce consuming need. She hummed with tension. It coiled inside of her, throbbing, insisting, making her feel wild for release. "I need you," she choked. "Need you to make love to me."

"I am," he said, as his fingers pressed deep.

She bucked against his hand, frantic, and frustrated. "Not like this. I want you, your body, your skin, in bed, on me." She'd go mad if she didn't have him soon. "Let's go inside," she whispered, licking her lip, her mouth dry, heart hammering. "Now."

"And what shall we do there?" he asked.

She gave her head a shake, dizzy, dazed. "Everything."

The corner of his mouth lifted. "This is only day three, *laeela*. We're to draw the pleasure out...make you wait."

"I waited all day for you!" she protested.

"Pleasure can't be rushed."

"Oh, I think it can. You've already made me half mad." She sat up, and pulled him forward to kiss him deeply, drawing his breath into her, opening her mouth to him, welcoming the tip of his tongue, sucking on the tip even as he thrust his fingers into her. She was so close to shattering, so close that she was afraid he'd stop, and walk away, and leave her aching. "I need you," she whispered against his mouth, frantic for him, frantic for release.

"You have me," he answered, his hands where she needed them, his mouth on hers, his tongue answering hers.

Her fingers curled into his crisp hair. Her nails pressed against his scalp. She leaned into him, pressing her breasts to his chest, letting her hips move, grinding against his hand. She was wanton but he felt good and tasted good and right now, she felt alive, and hungry for life, which was so different from how she'd felt this past year.

To go from dead to life…

To feel beautiful, and powerful…

He brought her to a climax, and she cried out as she shattered against him. She tipped her head against his, panting in release.

She should be horrified. Instead she felt strong. Hopeful. Jemma opened her eyes, looked into his. "What have you done to me?" she whispered.

"I'm just making sure you're satisfied," he said, kissing her.

"I'm satisfied," she said, still breathless. "But what about you?"

"I'm good."

"Yes," she agreed. "You are." And he did feel good. He felt solid and real and permanent in the best sort of way. "Can we now go to the bedroom?"

He kissed her again, and smoothed her hair back from her face. "I wish I could. Unfortunately, I have another conference call and this one is going to take a while. The staff knows to serve you dinner when you're hungry. Don't wait for me."

"Not again!"

"I know it's frustrating but it's important. Trust me." His dark eyes held hers, searching hers. "Do you believe me?"

She sighed, and nodded, because she did believe him. She couldn't imagine him lying to her. Not now. Not ever. "Yes."

"Just know that I will come to you tonight in the Amethyst Chamber, as soon as I can."

"I don't want to go there without you."

"But I will be there, *laeela*. I promise. Soon."

She ate dinner alone in the Amethyst Chamber, the walls painted a deep plum, and then stenciled in gold. The low wooden bed was framed with long embroidered silk curtains in shades of purple and plum, with violet hued pillows and a silk coverlet decorating the bed.

She didn't belong here, she thought, finishing her dinner, and returning the dishes to the tray by the door.

She didn't belong in Saidia and she didn't belong in Mikael's life. When she was with him, he distracted her from reality, making her forget what was true and important.

Like her work, and her family.

Like getting back to London and to those who did love her.

It was good to be away from him this evening. It was good to have time to herself, to find herself, and most of all, to remember how she'd come to be here, at the Bridal Palace, in the first place.

She'd been forced here. She'd been forced into this marriage. And she'd been forced to surrender to Sheikh Karim.

She had to remember that. Had to remember the facts, and reality, next time Mikael showed up, and touched her, and kissed her and made her want nothing but him.

She fell asleep, with the light on, determined to be strong when he arrived. She would resist him this time. She wouldn't melt for him. She wouldn't ache or need or shatter in his hands. Not anymore. Never again.

As her eyes closed she counted the days and nights she'd been here. Tonight was the third night. That meant there were just five more and then she'd be free.

Jemma woke up, blinked. It was morning. She looked around, pushing her long hair back from her face, and tugging the strap of her filmy purple nightgown back up onto her shoulder.

She was alone.

Good.

Good, she silently insisted. She'd gone to bed alone so it shouldn't surprise her that she was the only person in the bed, but she'd dreamed about Mikael all night, dreamed of Mikael kissing her, making love to her, and it'd felt so real. She woke up feeling as if he had been there, with her.

But he wasn't. It was a figment of her imagination. A dream.

She stretched her arm out across the empty bed, suddenly terribly homesick.

Day four, she told herself. Just four more days, and four more nights, and she'd be home.

The thought should have pleased her, reassured her, instead her heart fell, and her eyes burned. She missed Mikael. She shouldn't miss him. She should hate him.

The wooden door to the en suite bath creaked. Jemma sat up, startled.

Mikael appeared in the doorway, wearing nothing but loose cotton pajama pants that hung deliciously low on his hip bones. He raked a hand through his dark hair, making muscles ripple in his arms and chest.

She stared at his lean flat abdomen, each muscle hard and distinct.

"You're awake," he said, walking toward her and giving her the most devastatingly wicked smile.

Her heart lurched. "Where did you come from?"

"The bathroom."

Her heart did another funny little tumble. Just looking at him made her feel a pang. She didn't understand why he did that to her. She frowned. "How?"

"I walked."

She made a face, rolling her eyes. "Yes, but when?"

"Just a few minutes ago."

Her mouth dried. Her pulse was doing crazy, wild things. "But you weren't here. I fell asleep waiting for you."

"You might have fallen asleep before I arrived, but I did

come to you last night. I slept with you last night. I promised you I'd be here, and I am." He drew back the covers and slid in next to her. "You don't remember last night?"

"No." She frowned. "Did we...do...things?"

He reached across the bed for her, dragged her toward him, tangling her bare legs in the covers. "No. Regretfully not. I just held you. And spent the night with an endless hard-on."

She laughed as he pulled her under him but her laughter died as he lowered his powerful body onto hers. He was hard now. His length pressed against her belly.

"It's back," she whispered breathlessly.

"That's because it never went away." He dipped his head and kissed the side of her neck.

She sighed and arched against him. His hips ground against hers. She pressed her hips up, rubbing against the tip of his thick shaft, wanting it, wanting him.

"You want me," he said, his voice a rasp in her ear.

She nodded as his mouth covered hers, and she wrapped her legs around his hips. She did want him. All of him. And not just the things he did to her, but the things he made her feel. "Yes," she said, because she needed this, needed to feel. It had been a year of so much sadness and confusion that she needed to feel something warm and good again.

Mikael was making her feel very warm and good.

"What shall I do to you?" he murmured, kissing her jaw, and then her chin, before brushing her mouth with his.

She reached up, and wound her arms around his neck, drawing his head down. "Everything."

They kissed for hours, kissing until they were both panting and damp and tangled in sheets. Jemma wanted more, but she also loved this, the intense need, the desire, the fierce pleasure of just wanting and being wanted.

Her body ached and throbbed, even as her heart ached and throbbed. And as Mikael kissed her, touched her, his hands lighting her on fire and keeping the flames burning, glowing, she began to think that this might not just be lust anymore.

This wasn't about sex, either. It was more than sex. More than desire. Something else was stirring to life but what it was, she didn't know, and wasn't ready to face. Wasn't sure she could.

"I have news for you," he murmured against her mouth, his hands tangled in her hair. He kissed her once more. "We should talk."

Jemma went still. "What is it?"

"Your mother." He shifted his weight and moved away from her, rolling onto his back. He grabbed a pillow and placed it under his head. "And she's not sick, so you don't need to look at me like that."

"Like what?" Jemma demanded, sitting up, and tugging her sheer nightgown down, hoping she was adequately covered.

"Like something terrible has happened to her. Nothing terrible has happened. What's happened is good."

"What's happened?"

"It isn't good for your mother to have so much stress. A woman of her age needs to have her own home. I think she will do better if she has her own place again."

"Of course she would. We would all like that for her. But it's a dream at this point."

"There's a turn of the century shore colonial in Keofferam in Old Greenwich that I think would suit her. It has a big wraparound porch, and a small caretaker's apartment over a detached garage for a housekeeper or nurse, should your mother one day require one. It's recently been renovated so your mother wouldn't have to do anything."

"Yes, that all sounds very lovely, but you can't buy property in that area for less than two million, and a home such as the one you describe would easily be upward of three million—"

"Almost four," he agreed, "but it's in pristine condition and has the high ceilings and elegant formal rooms she would enjoy."

Jemma reached for a pillow and drew it to her chest. "You sound as if you know her."

"I did meet her at your sister's wedding, but you forget, your mother and mine were very similar in background. It's not difficult to imagine the kind of home she would be comfortable in, so I can tell you now that the house is in escrow, and I've been assured it will close at the end of today, as the wired funds have already reached the bank. I had my Realtor purchase the house in your mother's maiden name, which apparently is her legal name again. No one can take it from her."

Jemma stared at him. "I don't understand."

"I think she's suffered enough, don't you?"

Jemma struggled to speak around the lump filling her throat. "But you hate the Copelands."

"I hate your father, but your mother shouldn't be punished for his crimes." He hesitated. "Nor should you. So I did what I thought was best. It is my gift to you—"

"It's too much. I can't accept—"

"You don't have to. The gift is in your mother's name. There's nothing you can do about it."

"She won't accept it."

"She has."

"What?"

"I have been communicating with your brother, Branson. He has assisted me with a few financial details."

"He would never do that!"

Mikael sat up, muscles tightening across his chest, rippling down the length of his bare, lean torso. "You don't think a son wants his mother safe? Protected?"

"I know Branson. He wouldn't allow you to do such a thing."

"He would, if he understood we had done it together."

Jemma grew still. "You told him about…us?"

"I told him you were here with me, and that I intended to make you my queen."

"And he was okay with that?"

Mikael nodded and lay back down, arms folding behind his head. "Better than okay. He was very pleased for both of us and offered to throw us a party in London, as soon as we could visit. I told him we'd be there soon, probably before the end of the month."

She squeezed the pillow tighter. "You sound so smug."

"You should be happy I helped her, not angry."

"You can't do these things, though."

"Why not? I am your husband. It's my duty to provide for you and your family."

"A family you hate."

"Things have changed. You are my wife, and my family now, and I seek to honor you, and your family—"

"But what happens when I leave here in four days? What happens when you send me back? You promised you would, if I wasn't happy—"

"Are you unhappy?"

Her mouth opened but no sound came out. Was she unhappy?

It was strange to be asked that question now, so bluntly, because no, she wasn't unhappy. She was actually happier than she'd been in months, maybe even years.

"That's not the point," she said, sliding off the bed to pace the room.

"It's not?"

"No." She paced back toward him, confused, frustrated, no longer sure of anything.

"Then what is the point? Because I thought I had eight days to prove to you that I could make you happy, and I am making you happy, so what is the problem?"

She threw out her hands. "This!" she cried, gesturing at the purple walls with gold stencil. "This," she added, plucking at the silk nightgown. "This," she said, pointing to the bed, where he lay so supremely confident and comfortable, looking every bit a king. "None of this is real. None of this is my real life. It's just a dream. It's surreal. It's not going to last!"

"Says who?" he asked tersely, revealing the first hint of impatience.

"Me!"

"And you are an expert on reality? You, with the model for a boyfriend and the plan to enter Saidia on a stolen passport?"

"It wasn't stolen, it was my sister's, and you're hateful to throw Damien in my face. You know I loved him, and you know he hurt me. And you're just jealous because you can bombard me with expensive gifts but you know deep down, you'll never be able to buy my love."

Jemma walked out, pushing through the doors to the central courtyard, and then on to the other side, through a door to the Chamber of Innocence. She grabbed an ivory robe from the bathroom, wrapped it around her, and then walked out, leaving the Bridal Palace in search of her own wing. Her rooms, the ones she'd been brought to on arriving at the Kasbah.

She was done with this stupid honeymoon game. Done being kept locked up like a kidnapped bride. She wanted out. She wanted to go home.

"Where do you think you're going?" Mikael's deep voice rang out behind her. "We're not done, *laeela*."

"I am."

"It doesn't work that way."

"Maybe not for you!"

"Or you," he retorted, scooping her up into his arms and dropping her over his shoulder. "You owe me eight days and nights, and we're only halfway through. I get four more, and I will take all four."

"I don't want to do this anymore!"

"Too bad." He was carrying her back the way she'd just come, walking swiftly, his arm anchored across the back of her legs, holding her in place. "This isn't a game. You don't get to run away when you're tired or your feelings are hurt. This is real, you and me. This is reality."

He'd kicked open a door down the hall and then kicked it closed behind him. The room was dark and yet he knew where he was going, crossing the floor with long sure strides to drop her unceremoniously on the bed.

She scrambled into a sitting position. "Get out."

"That's not happening."

"I want to be alone."

"That's not happening, either." He untied the sash at her waist, peeled the robe off her shoulders and reached for the hem of her nightgown.

She slapped at his hands. "Don't touch me!"

"That, my dear wife, *is* happening."

CHAPTER THIRTEEN

MIKAEL REACHED PAST Jemma and turned on the small glass lamp on the bedside table, flooding the room with soft ruby light. The bed beneath Jemma gleamed with luxurious red satin, while the large jeweled mirror on the ceiling reflected the silk-covered walls and the decadent satin sheets.

With an irritated flick, he yanked the hem of Jemma's violet nightgown up, pulling it over her head and then tossing the scrap of violet silk onto the floor, before kicking off his own pajama bottoms. "We don't need these anymore," he said flatly, "now that we're in the Crimson Chamber."

Jemma scrambled back on the bed. "You've lost your mind."

"Maybe. Or maybe I've lost all patience. I'm not sure which right now," he said, grabbing her ankle and pulling her back toward him.

Jemma sprawled back on the bed, her long dark hair spilling across the crimson satin, her green eyes flashing. She'd never looked more beautiful. He would have her now. No more games. She was his. He'd chosen her. Married her. She was his queen.

He stretched out over her, and settled his weight between her thighs, his arousal pressing against her core.

She was hot, wet and his length rubbed against her slick heat. It would be so easy to thrust into her, and take her.

So easy to prove to her how much she wanted him.

He knew she craved him physically.

He knew he could make her scream and climax. He could draw out the orgasm and make it last for hours, too.

But that wasn't the point. His expertise as a lover wasn't in question. His future as a husband was. His father might have failed as a husband, but Mikael wouldn't.

Mikael dropped his head, and kissed her neck just above her collarbone, and then kissed higher on her neck, at the spot beneath her ear. He kissed the hollow and then the earlobe. He caught her earlobe in his teeth, his teeth lightly scraping, his breath lightly blowing in her ear.

He felt her nipples pucker and harden against his chest. He released her wrists and stroked her arms, moving in toward her ribs to cup the sides of her breasts, her skin soft and warm and then he stroked out again until his hands covered hers, his fingers linking with hers.

He kissed the side of her jaw, kissed the pulse beating frantically in the hollow beneath her ear and then he covered her mouth with his and kissed her, deeply, his tongue thrusting into her mouth, probing, possessing.

Her thighs parted wider for him. Her hips arched, her body rocking up against him.

"You aren't really angry because I helped your mother," he said, lifting his head to look down into her face. The paleness in her face was gone. Her cheeks flushed pink. She wanted him. "You're angry because you're afraid. You're angry because you're afraid these gifts—particularly this gift to your mother—will trap you in Saidia, with me."

Her eyes widened and she bit down into her lower lip.

He was right. That was her fear.

His chest grew tight. He felt an unaccountable pang, the pang eerily reminiscent of the ache and loss he'd felt after his mother left Saidia all those years ago. "*Laeela*, I made you a promise. You give me eight days and nights, and I will not keep you here against your will—"

"It's not you I'm afraid of," she interrupted. "It's me. I believe you will let me go. I believe you will put me on a plane should I request it. But I'm afraid that I might not request it, might not insist on it, and then everything that is uniquely me and mine, everything that I have worked so hard for all these years, will be gone."

"But if you remain here, you gain a new identity and a new life."

"As *your* wife. But I won't be anyone without you, and I vowed years ago to never be dependent on a man, much less a powerful man, and here in Saidia, I will be completely dependent on you."

"Is that such a bad thing if the powerful man is a just man?"

Her eyes turned liquid and she swallowed hard. "You already make my heart ache."

"I think we would make a good team, *laeela.*"

She struggled to smile. "Maybe you should just make love to me."

He dipped his head, kissed her lips. "Good idea. So what do you want, my beautiful bride? How can I please you today?"

"You," she said. "I just want you."

Jemma saw heat flare in Mikael's eyes and felt him harden against her.

She rocked her hips up, savoring the sensation of him against her. He was hard and warm, so warm, and she couldn't remember ever wanting anyone like this. "Make love to me, Mikael," she added, wrapping her arms around his neck and sinking her fingers into his crisp hair. "I need you."

His mouth covered hers, his tongue parting her lips to take her mouth even as he thrust smoothly, deeply into her body, filling her, stretching her.

He felt unbelievable.

She felt unbelievable.

Jemma's eyes burned and her chest ached, emotion bubbling up inside of her. Her arms slid down around his shoulders to hold him tighter. He was big and powerful and yet he fit her, and felt perfect to her.

Mikael kissed her, drawing her tongue into his mouth, sucking the tip even as he buried himself deeper into her body. She welcomed his weight and the fullness that stole her breath, and then he began to move. His lean sculpted hips dipped and he pressed deeper, then withdrew, only to stroke deep into her again.

She sighed and arched as he hit a spot inside her that tingled with pleasure. "More," she said, pressing up against him as he drove into her.

"I don't want to hurt you."

"It doesn't hurt. It feels so good." And it was true. It felt delicious everywhere. She felt delicious. Everything inside her was warm and sweet and bright. She felt like sunshine and honey, orange and spice and each stroke made her sigh a little deeper, and press against him a little harder.

"Don't stop," she whispered, meeting each of his thrusts, needing the friction, feeling the tension build. Each stroke of his body made her nerve endings tense, tighten, tingle.

He drove into her faster, increasing the rhythm. She loved the rhythm, the deep hard thrusts, the slickness of their bodies together, the warmth of his chest against hers. She could smell the scent of him, and them together, and it smelled right, felt right, more right than anything she'd ever felt before.

It didn't make sense, but then, none of this made sense and maybe passion never did.

The teasing tension within her quickened, sharpened, becoming bigger, and more powerful.

She panted and strained against him, wanting to come, not sure she could come and then he slipped his hand between them, stroking her even as he thrust hard into her wet tight body.

She wasn't prepared for the intensity of the orgasm and she screamed his name as he continued to stroke her, pushing her over the edge, her control shattering, her body climaxing, convulsively tightening around him.

He tensed, strained, his big powerful body arching as he buried himself deep inside her. She was still convulsing around him, her body squeezing him. With a guttural cry, he pulled out, making sure he spilled his seed into the sheets and not her.

She rolled over on the bed, on to her back, eyes closed, still struggling to catch her breath. He followed, lying on his side, next to her, his hand settling low on her hip.

She floated, feeling blissfully relaxed, and yet also very aware of Mikael at her side. She could feel the pressure of his hand, the warmth of his skin, smell his masculine spicy scent, practically hear his steady heartbeat. He was more real to her right now than she was.

He'd become her world in four days. It was exactly as she'd feared.

Jemma opened her eyes to find Mikael looking at her, his dark eyes so beautiful but so impossible to read. "Yes?" she whispered, dazzled, dazed.

"How do you feel?"

She let out a soft laugh and she turned to him, moving into his arms to rest her face on his chest. She could hear his heartbeat, smell his scent.

He smelled good. He felt good. He felt perfect, really.

"Good," she said softly, smiling unsteadily, because her emotions were bubbling up high and fast. "Very, very good."

They slept for an hour like that and Jemma woke first, sleepily stirring but couldn't move as Mikael's arms were around her and his muscular thigh was tucked between hers.

She lifted her head, looked down at him. He was still asleep, his thick black lashes beautiful onyx crescents against the gold of his cheek.

He looked different asleep. Younger. Boyish. Just a man, not a sheikh.

She put her head back down and nestled closer, liking the weight of his arm, the texture of his skin. He felt right. Perfect.

Did other women feel this way after making love? She'd had sex before but it hadn't felt like this. Like something important had happened. Something significant.

Even now she felt the rippling of emotion, like aftershocks. Something inside her felt aware, awake. Stirred.

Was this love? It couldn't be. She had to be feeling merely the side effect of seduction, and passion, all the result of his expert lovemaking.

If that was the case, then why did her very heartbeat seem to repeat his name? *Mik-ael. Mik-ael. Mik-ael.*

A moment later, he shifted, rolling on to his back, carrying her on top of him. His hand tangled in her long hair, and he parted her thighs, pushing her down against his hips. He was hard again, his erection rubbing against her. "Are you too sore to let me love you again?" he asked, his deep voice as husky and smoky as his dark eyes.

"No."

He lifted her, drawing her down on him, and with his hands on her hips, he helped her ride him, slow and deep, and then faster as the pleasure built.

After they both came, she tumbled forward onto his chest, and he held her. Her eyes closed. She listened to the thud of his heart and breathed him in.

He felt so good. He made her feel safe. *Happy.*

She was happy. This was the best place she'd been in months, emotionally, physically. In years.

Silence stretched between them, silence and a tingling awareness that everything had changed.

Mikael breathed in, out, and she traveled with his breath, his chest lifting her, carrying her.

That's how it'd been when they were joined. She'd felt lifted, carried, supported.

It had been so intimate, and yet it wasn't just sex. It felt like so much more, maybe because it had been so intense, and so physical, it'd demanded all of her, and she'd surrendered.

Making love to him, she gave herself up to him, offering him everything—her body, her mind, her emotions…her heart.

Why her heart? It made no sense. Jemma protected her heart. She'd learned it was necessary for survival. And yet in one morning of lovemaking, she'd dropped her defenses, lost her boundaries and become someone else. Or something else.

Changed.

There was that word again. She couldn't help going back to it. Changed. Altered. Shattered.

Confused.

How could sex do that? How could sensation be so powerful? She didn't understand and yet everything inside her felt open. Her heart felt open.

She pressed her palm to his chest, savoring the steady thud of his heart. "Did you really buy my mother a house?" she asked huskily.

His fingers played with her hair, twisting the long strands. "I will go check and see if the escrow has closed. I expect it will have."

"And then it will be hers?"

"And hers alone," he agreed.

Jemma hesitated. "Even if I leave here in four days?"

"No one can take it from her."

Jemma was profoundly moved, but also troubled. "I don't know what to say. I know I should thank you—"

"You don't need to thank me. I didn't buy it for you. I did it for her."

"You don't even know her."

"I met her at Morgan's wedding. She was kind to me. I liked her. She reminded me of my mother."

Mikael left her to check on the status of the house and Jemma showered and dressed, slipping into the long ruby beaded skirt and matching ruby top laid out on the bed. Breakfast was served in the courtyard. She'd just sat down and had her first coffee when Mikael returned.

"Escrow closed. The paperwork has been signed. The house is hers," he said, taking the chair opposite Jemma's.

"Thank you," Jemma said. "Thank you for caring for her. Thank you for wanting the best for her."

"I do for her what I should have done for my mother." His brow furrowed, and his voice dropped, cracking. "I was not good to my mother. I failed her, and I will carry that pain, and that shame, with me forever."

She reached across the table, and covered his hand with hers. "How did you fail her? What did you do?"

"Nothing. That is what I did. Absolutely nothing."

"I don't understand."

"When I explain, you'll be appalled. And you should be. My behavior was selfish and it still disgusts me, but it's too late to fix things. Too late to make amends."

Jemma winced at his sharp tone, his voice laced with self-loathing and scorn. "Explain to me."

"I was twenty-two when I learned the truth about my father and mother, that my father had lied to her, and had destroyed their wedding contract so he could take another wife. I was furious with my father," he said, "but I'd lost my mother years ago, when I was just a boy, eleven, and I was terrified of losing my father, too. He had so many other children, so many other sons he could admire and love, and so I pretended I didn't know the truth about the divorce. I pretended that I didn't know who my father was—a liar, a cheat—and I acted as if my father was this wonderful man."

"You were his son," she said. "You were showing him respect."

"My father had turned his back on my mother. I understood he expected me to do the same. And so I did, even when she came to me on my twenty-fifth birthday, asking for help. She was nervous about her future. She wanted financial assistance, and advice. She was worried she wasn't managing her money well. She was worried she'd run out if she didn't have the right investments."

"Did you help her?"

"No."

"No?"

His jaw tightened. "I took her to coffee and told her I couldn't help her, that she'd created this situation by leaving my father. I told her there was nothing I could do." Mikael averted his face, staring off across the courtyard, his features set. "She didn't cry. She didn't beg. She just folded up her papers and slipped them back into her purse, then kissed me, and left."

Jemma's eyes burned. "You were young."

"I wasn't young. I was angry." He turned to look at her, expression fierce. "I wanted to punish her for leaving me all those years ago, for leaving me with a father who barely remembered me because he had so many wives and sons and daughters, all clamoring for his attention. So I rejected her, wanting her to hurt as I had hurt."

Silence stretched.

He drew a deep, rough breath. "I never did help her with her investments, even though I had degrees in finance and economics. Even though I worked in London as an institutional investor until I was nearly thirty." Mikael shifted restlessly. "I knew money. I knew how to make money. And I could have aided her, protected her, but I didn't. So she went to your father and trusted him, and we all know how that turned out."

"But she didn't go to my father until after Morgan's wedding. At least, that's what I thought you said."

"Yes. But she went to him because she'd made some bad investments earlier, and your father promised he could do impossible things with what capital she had left. He could get her an incredible return on her investment with him, and so she gave him everything. Everything. And he stole it all."

Jemma winced, sickened all over again by her father's betrayal. "That's on his head, not yours."

Mikael turned his head, looked at her from beneath his dense black lashes. "My mother should have died of old age, comfortable in her American home. But she lost her home, along with her nest egg. Heartbroken, and terrified, she took her life. Hung herself in the hall of her home the day she was to be evicted."

Jemma stared at him, aghast. "She killed herself?"

He nodded. His jaw worked, and he ran a hand down his throat, as if trying to find the words. "She was just fifty-four," he said when he could finally speak again. "But she'd lost her home…again. She knew she couldn't go to my father. She was afraid to come to me. We were still rebuilding our relationship and she was afraid I'd be disappointed in her, so she panicked. She did what she thought was the best answer for all."

"I'm so sorry."

"I still have that last note, the note she left, saying she was sorry, and begging me to forgive her for being stupid and weak."

He turned his head abruptly but not before Jemma saw the suffering in his eyes.

For several moments there was just silence, an endless, impossible silence heavy with grief.

Jemma reached out and placed her hand over his. "People make mistakes," she whispered.

"It's my fault she died," he said. "At first I blamed my father, and your father, but I am the one responsible for this. I did this to her. I rejected her. Refused her. I left her no hope—"

"Would you have helped her if she came to you about her house, Mikael?" she interrupted, leaving her seat and moving around the table to kneel before him. "If she'd told you her situation, that she had nowhere to go, and no way to pay her bills, would you have taken care of her?"

"*Yes.*"

"Are you sure? Or is that what you say now?"

He stiffened, shoulders squaring. His dark eyes burned down at her. "You don't think I would?"

"*I* know you would," she said, taking his hands, holding them tightly. "But do you? That's the important question. Because until you believe you would have helped her, you won't be able to forgive…you, her, or your father."

CHAPTER FOURTEEN

MIKAEL WAS DONE talking. He'd said far more than he'd intended to say but he was glad he'd told Jemma the truth. Glad she knew now who he was, and what he was. Better for her to know on the fourth day than the eighth. Better to give her all the facts up front, instead of blindsiding her at the end.

He rose from the table, drew her up to her feet. "I cannot think anymore, or talk anymore. I am talked out. I need diversion. What about you?"

"What do you have in mind?"

"You'll see."

She followed him back into the Crimson Chamber. The satin sheets had been changed, and freshly made, the bed lined with stacks of ruby-hued pillows.

A bright white light shone from the ceiling, onto a screen attached to the far wall.

He saw Jemma glance up at the light, and then saw the moment she realized it was actually a projector. "Is that what I think it is?" she asked, turning to him.

"Do you like movies?"

"Yes."

"I do, too. I thought maybe you could use a break from the pool and the sun and would enjoy a good film."

"I'd love it. But only if you stay with me. Otherwise I wouldn't enjoy it at all."

Jemma loved their afternoon at the movies in the Crimson Chamber. The dark red walls and rich burgundy and ruby pillows and cushions made the room feel like an elegant, and exotic, movie theatre. Staff brought them food during a break between the two films, a break Jemma laughingly called the "intermission," and then curled back up in Mikael's arms when the second film began.

He had to leave at the end of the second movie to check in with his staff. He kissed her before he left and promised to meet her for dinner in the courtyard. They were to dine outside tonight, inside the pink and turquoise tiled pavilion. "We'll go to the Turquoise Chamber tonight. You'll enjoy tonight," he told her, kissing her again.

"I've enjoyed every night," she answered truthfully, smiling up at him.

She arrived in the courtyard that evening before he did, dressed in the filmy turquoise kaftan that had been laid out for her.

The kaftan was long, reaching her ankles and it swished as she walked, clinging to her stomach, hips and thighs.

Jemma wandered around the grand courtyard, admiring the large blue tiled pool lit by blue and pink lights, and pausing to smell the sweet fragrant lilies and roses that grew in clusters in enormous glazed pots.

She was glad she'd arrived in the courtyard before Mikael. She enjoyed having this moment to herself, liked the excitement bubbling within her, and the sense of anticipation.

She'd enjoyed this afternoon with Mikael. She'd found it hard to concentrate on the movies, though, with him there, at her side. She'd wanted him to make love to her, but he hadn't. He'd held her, and kissed her several times, but he'd otherwise shown admirable restraint.

She, on the other hand, wanted to be touched. She'd curled at his side, pretending to watch the movie when all she really wanted was touch. She was beginning to feel addicted to pleasure. Or was she addicted to him? She didn't know, wasn't sure how she could know.

Jemma felt a tingle down her spine. She wasn't alone anymore. She knew Mikael had arrived even before she turned to see him.

Slowly she faced him. He was standing at the far end of the pool, watching her. "That color suits you," he said.

Suddenly the courtyard hummed with energy. She felt the same electric surge in her veins, her heart racing, too.

He was wearing black trousers and a white linen shirt and he looked handsome and virile and confident.

Her husband. Her king.

She smiled, amused by the thought, but the thought took hold. He might very well be a good husband for her. He seemed to be a good king.

A servant appeared with a tray of cocktails and together Jemma and Mikael walked around the courtyard, with Mikael pointing out various plants that had significance, whether due to age, or relationship to the Kasbah.

"The date palms were for a great-grandmother, and the citrus trees were for my grandmother. The trees are replaced every ten to fifteen years, depending on their maturity and fruit production. My mother loved pink roses, so those were for her." Mikael smiled at her. "What shall we plant in your honor? What is your favorite flower?"

She shook her head. "I think it's all perfect just the way it is. I wouldn't change anything."

"You don't want to be immortalized in the Bridal Palace's garden?" he asked.

She knew he was teasing her. She could see it in his eyes and the quirk of his mouth and she felt a bubble of warmth inside her.

She was happy.

That's why she felt different…why everything seemed different. The happiness explained the bright sparks in her head and in her eyes. The happiness made her tingle, and her insides fizz.

It wasn't the desert heat temperatures heating her, warming her, but happiness. And she was happy because of him. Happy because she cared about him. And cared maybe more than she should.

They made love in the Turquoise Chamber and fell asleep tangled together, skin damp, limbs intertwined.

Jemma woke first, it was early.

Day five, she thought. She would be here for only three more days.

She counted the nights in her head, remembering the colors...

White the first night in the Chamber of Innocence, and then Topaz, Amethyst, Ruby or Crimson, and then last night was Turquoise.

Where would they go tonight? To the Emerald Chamber? Sapphire?

Did it even matter?

She had to leave. Had to return to London. Didn't she?

Confused by her conflicting thoughts, Jemma quietly left the bed and stepped outside to the courtyard. It was still early. The sun was just rising and the temperature felt cool, the early morning painted the palest pink and yellow.

Jemma's maid appeared in the courtyard with coffee and a tray of breakfast pastries. Jemma refused the pastries but sipped the coffee in a chair near the tranquil pool, listening to the chirp of birds nesting high above in the palm fronds.

Mikael appeared in the doorway a half hour later. He'd showered and dressed and was wearing his robes. "I need to go to Ketama," he said, approaching her to drop a kiss on the top of her head. "I will be back tonight. I wouldn't leave if I didn't have to."

She tipped her face up to him, frowning at the amount of time he'd be traveling, first by camel, and then by car. "Won't it take you all day to get there?"

He kissed her again, this time on her brow. "I have a helicopter here. The pilot's ready. If we leave now, I'll be back this evening."

"And you have to go?"

"Yes," he said, sounding very decisive.

"Be careful," she said.

He kissed her one last time, this time on the lips. "Always."

It seemed as if it would be a long day with Mikael gone, but Jemma's maid led her to the Emerald Chamber, with the wall of antique leather-bound books.

Jemma studied the spines, delighted to discover that many were in English, and many were written by her favorite English authors. Charles Dickens, Thomas Hardy, Jane Austen, the Bronte sisters, E.M. Forster, and more.

Jemma selected *Mansfield Park* by Jane Austen and curled up in bed to read. She read the afternoon away and was still reading when the maid appeared to help Jemma dress for dinner.

"Is His Highness back?" Jemma asked, reluctantly putting the book down.

The maid shook her head. "No."

"Then why do I need to dress for dinner? Can't I have dinner here, in bed?"

Jemma finished the novel over dessert and promptly began *Sense and Sensibility* but ended up falling asleep over it.

She was still asleep, holding the novel, when Mikael arrived at midnight.

He stood over the bed for a moment watching her before carefully plucking the book from her hand, drawing the covers up to her shoulder, and turning the lamp out next to the bed.

He showered in the marble bathroom and then after drying off, joined her in bed. He was naked. But then, so was she.

Jemma woke up in the night and reached out to her side, relieved and delighted to discover Mikael there.

She moved toward him, and he opened his arms to her, drawing her close.

She pressed her face to his warm chest, breathing in his scent. He was back and he felt good and smelled good and she lifted her face to his, offering her lips. He kissed her, taking her mouth and then rolling her onto her back, to thrust deep inside her.

She wrapped her legs around his hips, taking all of him, wanting to hold him as close as possible, aware that things were changing. She was changing.

She...loved...him.

She loved him.

All of a sudden it made sense. She was happy because she was in love.

They fell back asleep and then woke up sometime in the morning to make love again. This time Jemma didn't fall back asleep but slipped from bed to head to the bathroom to shower.

Mikael watched Jemma cross the bedroom, naked, her beautiful body so familiar to him now.

Maybe that's why his chest felt heavy and tight as he watched her disappear into the bathroom.

Maybe that's why sex had felt different last night and this morning.

Maybe it's because she was familiar to him. Important to him.

But she was different, too, he thought. She hadn't merely been in his arms, but with him...in him...which didn't make sense, as it was his body filling hers, but somehow she'd gotten inside of him. He had felt *her*, feeling her not just with his body but his heart.

The emotions and sensations had made the sex more intense.

She'd felt so alive beneath him, so fierce and fragile, so beautiful that he couldn't get close enough to her, and he'd tried, God knew he'd tried.

Slow, deep strokes, hands holding her down, and still so he could kiss her, ravish her, draw her all the way into him.

And it hadn't been enough. He couldn't get enough. Even after one, two orgasms…hers, his.

Before, when he'd pleasured her, he'd wanted to blow her mind, enslave her through passion, make her yield to him. Belong to him. If she was going to be his, she should be happy with him.

But today it'd been something else.

There had been more heat than ever before but the heat wasn't about skin or erotic zones. It wasn't about the orgasm, either.

It was her. Wanting her. Holding her. Being with her.

And he could have sworn she'd been into him. Not the act. Not the friction and tension, not the positions, either.

Somehow the game of seduction had changed and become something more. More real, more honest, more raw. Suddenly, the stakes seemed higher than ever. Could he make Jemma happy? Could he keep her here with him in Saidia?

And if he could, was it fair to her? Or to those in her family?

Mikael threw back the covers, and headed for the bathroom where he could hear Jemma showering.

Hot steam filled the white marble bath, thick fragrant clouds hanging in the air.

He could just make her out through the wisps, her long hair piled high on her head, her hands on her breasts, spreading the bath gel across her lovely pale skin. He hardened, wanting her, craving her again.

He should be sated by now. He should have had his fill.

How many times did a man need a woman?

And yet watching her dark head dip, as she looked down her long, slim torso, to the suds running from her breasts to her belly, his body tightened, his arousal surging upright.

He couldn't stay away. He needed her. Again. He'd have her, too.

Mikael pushed open the glass door to the sunken shower, steam rising, embracing him.

Jemma turned toward him, startled, her lips parting in surprise.

Her eyes, those lips, her face...

Hunger raced through him. Hunger and the need to have her, hold her, keep her. He reached for her, and pushing her back against the wet marble wall, pressed his chest to hers, feeling the slippery film of soap suds between them, skin slick, enticing.

He rubbed his chest across her soft breasts and felt her nipples pebble. He inhaled sharply, as something wrenched in his chest.

This was new, this need. He didn't understand it. Didn't understand this desire. It was bigger than before, fiercer, wild in a way that baffled him, knocking him off balance.

Sex did not confuse him.

Women did not confuse him.

But he was confused now.

Confused by Jemma with the green eyes and soft lips and sweetness that pierced his heart and made him want to please her and protect her, keeping her safe, keeping her from harm's way.

With the water coursing down she lifted her face to his and he couldn't resist her lips. His head dropped, his mouth slanting across hers, hands framing her face.

Beautiful Jemma.

Beautiful woman.

Beautiful heart.

His chest burned. His eyes stung. He leaned in, crowding her, trying to take the upper hand. He was the master here. He was in control. He would prove this was just sex.

He broke off the kiss and turned her around, pressing her breasts to the warm slick marble even as he pulled her bottom toward him. His hand reached between her legs, finding her softness, and heat. He pushed up against her bottom, stroking her, feeling her legs quiver as his body strained against her.

She was so hot, so wet. He wanted to bury himself in her,

wanted to have her surround him, hot and tight, but he was too rough right now, and he couldn't hurt her. Couldn't force her. She'd given him so much earlier, it would be wrong to just take her now—

"I'm waiting," she said, her voice husky, her hips rocking against him. "Stop teasing me. You know I want you."

The sex was hot and Jemma left the shower satisfied, but Mikael did not.

That wasn't right, taking her like that. But was bringing her to the Kasbah in the first place right? He'd kidnapped a foreign woman. Forced her to marry him.

He toweled off slowly, guilt beginning to eat at him, even as a little voice in his head whispered, *you are wrong. This is wrong.*

He didn't like the little voice, didn't want the little voice. The voice represented the past, and weakness. But Karims must be strong. Karims must be above the law.

Mikael spent several hours at his desk on phone calls and in meetings before changing into comfortable clothes to meet Jemma for dinner in the grand courtyard. The pavilions and pools had been lit with sapphire and pink lights.

Jemma wore a long deep blue kaftan with silver and gold embroidery. The inky color of her dress made her green eyes even more brilliant. He sat across from her at dinner to see her, but the table between them meant he couldn't touch her too easily.

Instead he watched her face and her eyes as she talked during their meal. Her green eyes shimmered when she laughed. She laughed easily, her expression dancing.

She was so warm. And good. She deserved good things, and good people.

He was not a good person.

Powerful, yes. Wealthy, exceptionally so. But good? No.

During dessert and coffee he remembered he had a gift for her, and he pulled the velvet box from the pocket in his robe.

"For you," he said, handing her the box.

She looked up at him, dark winged eyebrows lifting higher. "You have to stop."

"Never."

She laughed, eyes dancing. "Fine. I tried. I won't fight you anymore because a gift now and then is rather nice." Then she opened the box, lifted the stunning sapphire earrings out, jaw dropping in awe. "Oh," she whispered, giving one earring a slight shake. "These, my husband, are absolutely stunning."

Mikael's lips curved, and yet on the inside he grew very still.

My husband, she'd said. Not sarcastically, or angrily. But kindly. Warmly.

It made his chest tighten and ache. He tried very hard to be a good king, but that didn't make him deserving of a woman like Jemma.

"Be careful," he said to her, leaning across the table and kissing her gently. "Be careful of wolves in sheep's clothing."

She smiled into his eyes as her hand reached up to cup his face. "I know of no sheep. Just wolves. And hawks. And scary desert scorpions and snakes."

He stared into her eyes an extra moment, taking her in, feeling the impact of her beauty and warmth. "I could very well be one of those poisonous scorpions or snakes."

"You could." She rubbed his jaw, fingernails scratching lightly along his stubble before sitting back. "But I don't think so. I've seen who you are. You're a man determined to restore honor to your country, and preserve tradition. You are protective of women, just look at how you've treated me, and provided for my mother."

"Because I failed to provide for mine."

"You're making amends."

"Too late, though, for her."

He rose abruptly from the table, unable to sit another moment, and extended his hand to her. "Come with me."

He led her to the enormous bed in the Sapphire Chamber, and stripped her of her gown and delicate silk bra and thong before kissing her and making love to her. The lovemaking was slow, sensual, lasting for hours.

Satiated, Jemma remained in Mikael's arms. He held her closely and Jemma sighed, feeling secure.

He felt right to her. Being with him felt good. The humiliation and shame of the past year couldn't hurt her when she was in his arms. Damien's rejection no longer mattered. Damien wasn't anything but a lousy model, a spineless man. She smiled to herself, feeling safe…content…loved.

Mikael had somehow made her feel whole again, and strong.

Saidia wasn't home, but Mikael could be. And while he hadn't said words of love, he'd given her something else. His commitment. His promise.

She trusted his word. She cherished his vows because he was a man of his word, and a man who took his commitments seriously.

This, she thought, wrapping her arms over his, this is what she needed. This is who she wanted. This was her future.

In the morning, Jemma woke slowly, feeling deliciously lazy, and deeply rested. Eyes still closed, she let herself breathe and float. At least, it felt as if she were floating. Everything inside her was warmth and light. Easy.

The world was good.

Life was better.

Her lashes fluttered, a butterfly kiss, and she opened her eyes, and saw Mikael lying next to her. She smiled with pleasure. She loved sleeping with him, loved having him there with her all night.

She was quite attracted to this man.

"Good morning, *laeela*," Mikael said, eyes still closed, his voice deep and husky with sleep.

"You're awake," she said, pleased.

"No. I'm still sleeping," he said, his voice still with that lovely gravelly growl she found enormously sexy. "My eyes are shut."

"Then how did you know I was awake?" she asked, amused, propping her head on her hand.

"I could feel you watching me."

"Then you are awake."

He sighed. His beautiful dark eyes opened, and he looked at her, black eyebrow lifting. "*Now* I am."

She grinned. "Hi."

He sighed again, heavily, but his eyes glinted. "Hello."

Jemma laughed softly. He was acting put out but he wasn't really. "How did you sleep?" she asked him.

"Well. And you?"

"Exceedingly well."

"You like our fresh desert air."

"No, I like you. Being held by you." She felt bold, but she didn't care. How could she be shy around him when he made her feel so beautiful and strong? "That's three nights you've stayed with me, all through the night."

"I am committed to your pleasure."

"You most certainly are," she agreed, hiding her smile as she studied his hard, handsome features. Such a striking face. All strong lines and edges and then that soft curve of lip... lower, upper. He was so nice to look at. "I appreciate your commitment."

A deep groove formed next to his mouth. His lips quirked. "You are shameless."

"You've only yourself to blame, Your Highness. You've made me shameless."

He reached out to brush long strands of hair from her brow, gently pushing them back from her face, his thumb easing across her forehead in a soft caress. "Have I? How?"

Just that light touch sent shivers through her, and darts of pleasure to her breasts and between her thighs. Senses stirred, she exhaled slowly, carefully, her thoughts tangling. It was hard to think when Mikael touched her. "How can I feel shame when everything we do together makes me feel wonderful, and powerful?"

"Sex makes you feel powerful?"

She frowned. It didn't sound right, not phrased like that. "I'm sure great sex makes lots of people feel powerful, but I wasn't referring to sex in general, but sex with you." She frowned again. Because that didn't sound right, either. She wasn't having sex with Mikael. She was making love with Mikael. She was loving Mikael.

She was most definitely *in love* with Mikael. She wished she could tell him. Wished she knew how to tell him that the pleasure she felt with him wasn't merely sexual. It wasn't just physical. Her pleasure was in her heart, and soul.

She looked into his eyes, and she flashed back to that first day on the desert dunes when she'd been melting inside the fur coat and high boots. He'd had the same intense expression in his dark eyes and she'd been afraid...

Now she was afraid again, but for a different reason. She couldn't imagine being happy without him.

"Kiss me," she whispered, reaching up to his face, placing her hand against his hard, high cheekbone as she pressed her lips to his. "Possess me. Remind me that I'm your wife and queen."

His wife and queen.

Mikael stared blindly out through the glass doors, seeing nothing of his courtyard, and seeing only Jemma's face.

He, who was so good at creating order, structure, and discipline, hadn't planned on falling in love with her. He hadn't planned on wanting her, or needing her, not the way he wanted her and needed her.

He'd married her out of duty and responsibility but suddenly his marriage was one of love. Trust. *Respect.*

He'd known he was growing fond of her these past few days. He'd known he was getting attached, too. It hadn't troubled him. At least, he hadn't let it trouble him. He would only allow himself to think of one thing—doing what was right for Saidia. But now he felt a wash of shame. This was wrong chaining her here, to him. He couldn't trap her in Saidia. He couldn't do it to her. She deserved so much better than this.

Jemma was in her sapphire room, sitting on the floor, painting her toenails when Mikael entered a half hour later.

He didn't knock. But then, he hadn't knocked on the door in days, taking it for granted that her room was his. That she was his. He was right. It hadn't even taken eight days to fall in love with him. She'd given him her heart far earlier…maybe even that first day they'd met, when she'd been modeling on the sand dunes.

He silently watched her paint her pinky toe a foamy mint green. She glanced up at him, smiling. "I remember how much you like the color green."

"I don't remember that at all."

"You said you loved my eyes."

"Yes, your eyes. Not green toenails."

Jemma laughed and dipped the brush into the bottle for more polish. "Are you sure that's what you said? I worry about your memory."

"I worry about you and facts."

She grinned, happy. Ridiculously happy. Everything inside her bubbled up warm, and hopeful. Her heart felt good. Mikael made her feel good. And safe. *Loved.* He might not say the words the way she wanted to hear them, but she felt his love in his actions. She felt his affection and love in the way he touched her, and the warmth and passion with which he kissed her. She saw it in the amusement in his eyes as they talked, teasing, bantering. The fact that he would banter with her, and laugh with her, said it all.

Lips curving, she added a second coat to the pinky toe, before capping the bottle of polish and setting it aside. She tipped her head back to look up into his beautiful face, with those dark, mysterious and oh so sexy eyes. "What can I do for you this beautiful day, my love?"

The hint of amusement died from his eyes, his expression

shuttering, his jaw hardening. It was a subtle shift. Someone else might not have picked up on the change, but she did. Jemma had spent so much time studying him these past eight days that even the narrowing of his eyes didn't go unnoticed.

"There is nothing you need to do. It's all been done," he said.

"It can't *all* be done," she said, noting the change, but trying to tease him. "The Kama Sutra refers to hundreds of positions, and we've only tried—" she scrunched her eyes closed, as if thinking very hard "Four or five?"

"I think you've practiced plenty."

She feigned shock. "You're sick of sex?"

His smile was crooked. "No, but I think we need to get out. Go and do something. I've a picnic packed. Get your suit. We're heading to the beach."

"Camels to the beach? Now that would be interesting."

His mouth quirked, reluctantly amused. "We'll take the helicopter to Truka, and then my car to the beach town of Tagadir."

In the helicopter, on the way to Truka, Mikael explained that the Karim family owned miles of a beautiful private beach in the ancient resort town of Tagadir. There had once been an elegant nineteenth century villa in Tagadir, but the villa had been torn down by Mikael's father who planned to build a new one, but the new one was never constructed. However, the beach was still there, with its soft white sand and beautiful warm water.

They reached the entrance to the Karim estate just after noon, passing through tall black, wrought iron gates. The long driveway toward the water was bordered with blooming hibiscus hedges in pinks and bright corals, but on reaching the end of the drive, right where one would expect to see a grand building, there was nothing but the ruins of a cement foundation, with stone steps leading down to the beach.

The driver delivered the picnic basket and blankets to the beach and then returned to the car. Jemma stood on the last step and surveyed the private cove. A small, but elegant stone pavilion rose from the sand. Otherwise there was nothing. The beach truly was lovely, and private.

After lunch, Mikael and Jemma swam. They dried out on their blanket and then returned to the water to cool off when the sun became too fierce. Mikael was back on the blanket now, watching Jemma float and splash.

Her skin glowed golden after these past few days lounging at the Kasbah pool. The touch of gold in her skin brought out the green of her eyes. In her white bikini she was beyond stunning.

He watched as she waded in, stepping from the surf to wring the water from her long dark hair.

He loved looking at her and talking to her and making love to her. He loved her company and enjoyed her laughter. The laughter was good, and needed. He had a tendency to be silent and stern but she brought out a more playful side in him. He hadn't always been hard.

Loving Jemma had opened him up, softened his heart.

He needed to send her home, back to her family, back to those who loved her and wanted what was best for her like her mother, and Branson, her brother, and the sisters who all adored Jemma.

Mikael wasn't sure that Jemma would understand. He hoped she wouldn't take his decision as a rejection. He wasn't rejecting her, but protecting her.

This was the time he could return her to her people, without shame or stigma. After the eight days and nights, before the official sixteen days of honeymoon ended.

He couldn't wait, either. He didn't want her to become too attached. He didn't want her to confuse lust and love. She was dazzled by pleasure, seduced by endorphins and chemicals. Orgasm tricked women's brains, flooding them with chemicals that made them attach...feel...need.

There was a reason Saidia men made love to their captive brides for eight days without ceasing. The sex, the pleasure, it was a drug. The frequent and intense orgasms helped the woman bond to her man so by the end of the honeymoon, the bride didn't want to leave her groom. The bride had become attached, even addicted to her groom, craving his scent, his touch, his feel, and each coupling would reinforce the attachment, and aid in procreation.

Mikael knew all this. Jemma didn't.

It was time he told her.

She dashed across the hot sand to join him on the blanket. She was laughing as she tumbled down onto the blanket, dripping water on him, making him wet.

"Wicked girl," he said, reaching for her.

She wrinkled her nose at him, making fun of him. His chest grew hot and tight. He had to have her, needed to touch her. He slid his hand into the long damp strands of her hair, the sea making her hair gritty, and he rolled her onto her back, and settled over her, kissing her, drinking her in.

He could taste the salt water on her lips and the cool ocean on her breath and it heated his blood, making him hungry. He deepened the kiss, his tongue parting her lips. Mikael teased her tongue, stroking it, stroking her mouth, delving into it until he felt her shudder and arch against him.

He shifted, and leaned back on the blanket, and drew her on top of him, settling her slim hips between his thighs, so that his arousal pressed thickly against her.

Jemma sighed against his mouth, and he felt her yield to him, her body softening, shaping to his, her lovely full breasts crushed to his chest, her nipples peaked, hard, and he reached around to cup her bottom. She sighed again as he palmed her buttocks, his fingers kneading the smooth muscle. She groaned deep in her throat as he pressed her down against him, rubbing her pelvis against him, feeling her softness cup him. He nearly groaned, too.

She felt so good. He stroked her hips, her rounded bottom, her inner thighs, all while driving his tongue into her, an insistent rhythm that made her writhe helplessly against him, her body trembling in anticipation.

She strained to get even closer, her breath coming faster.

His hands slid up her thighs, until his fingers brushed the fabric of her bikini bottoms. She was hot, wet, and her heat scorched him. He rubbed across her, feeling her softness through the fabric, finding her sensitive spot.

Her eyes widened and she panted. He loved the way she did that…gasp, shudder, pant. She was so beautiful and sensual. He loved that she could forget her inhibitions and lose herself in him. In them.

He caressed her between her thighs again and again, feeling her grow hotter, wetter. She jerked, nerve endings exquisitely sensitized, and flung her head back, her eyes emerald, cheeks flushed. With her dark hair still wet and the halo of sun above them, she looked like a goddess from the sea and he had to have her, now.

He rolled her over onto her back, and tugged her damp bikini bottoms off of her. His thighs parted hers and he sank into the cradle of her hips, nudging her soft folds, eager to be inside her. His tip stroked her smooth, secret places, her creamy heat calling to him, drawing him in.

Mikael entered her with a thrust, slipping deeply inside her tight body.

He loved her the way he knew she liked to be loved—deep, slow, hard—and with his body he tried to say all the things he'd never be able to say in words.

That she mattered too much.

That she was too valuable.

That she deserved so much more than he could give.

CHAPTER FIFTEEN

JEMMA LAY IN his arms on the blanket in the sand, resting comfortably, happily. There was no place she'd rather be than here, in his arms, against his chest. "What day is this?" she asked, lifting her chin, to look at him.

"I think I've lost count," he said, smoothing her hair back from her brow.

She lifted a brow. "Really? I don't believe that for a minute."

"So what day is it?"

"Day eight. The last day and night of your half of our honeymoon."

She waited for him to say something. He didn't.

"Tonight you are still in control," she added, blushing a little. "But tomorrow I take over. Tomorrow I'm in charge for the next eight days and nights."

She smiled into his eyes, waiting impatiently for him to say something, something warm and sexy. Something encouraging. Something.

But he didn't speak. He just looked at her, his dark eyes somber, expression grave.

Her heart did a funny double beat. Nervous and uncomfortable, she chewed the inside of her lower lip. "You've gone awfully quiet," she murmured.

His jaw shifted, his lids dropping, hooding his eyes. "I have been thinking a great deal about tonight."

"So have I. I think it's time you let me pleasure you."

"I don't think there is going to be a tonight."

Jemma froze. Blinked.

"There is just…today," he added quietly.

For a second she couldn't breathe. She couldn't think. Couldn't do anything at all.

"I married you so you wouldn't have to remain in Haslam under house arrest for seven years. But the eight days are up. I have fulfilled my responsibility as a groom, and I can now return you to London, without losing face."

She still couldn't take it all in. She took his words apart, bit by bit, processing them. Digesting them.

He didn't want an eighth night. He didn't want to be married to her. He intended to put her on a plane for London.

She licked her lips, her mouth dry. Parched. "I'm confused," she whispered.

"I did what needed to be done," he said carefully, after an endless moment, a moment where the silence cut, wounded.

Jemma slowly pulled away, and then scooted away, and sat up. She crossed her legs, hiding herself. "You never intended to keep me as your wife?"

"It's not feasible. Nor realistic. My mother wasn't happy in Saidia. You wouldn't be happy here, not long term. You'd be better marrying an American or a European man. Someone Western with Western thought processes and beliefs."

"So all this time…these eight days and the past seven nights…what was it about? Just sex?"

He shrugged. "Please."

"But you said pleasure could lead to more. You said pleasure could lead to love."

"I was wrong."

She looked at him, then away, trying to ignore the panic in her head and the sickening rush of hurt and pain through her veins.

This wasn't happening, not now. She'd fallen in love with him and she'd given herself to him.

"Why?" she whispered, staring out at the white sandy beach

and the sea beyond. "Why do this to me? Why go through all the motions and seduce me and pleasure me and pretend to care? Pretend to want me?"

"I do care about you. I never had to pretend to want you. I still want you. I still desire you. But I've realized I care too much about you, to trap you here in Saidia. You need more than this desert and my palaces. You need the world you grew up in."

"This isn't about me," she said, interrupting him. "This is about your mother. It's about her relationship with your father, not about you and me." Jemma drew a rough, unsteady breath. "I am not your mother. I am not sheltered. I am not a naive young American girl thinking she's being swept off by Valentino. I've experienced hard things and known tremendous pressure, and public criticism, and personal shame. So don't think for me, and don't make decisions for me, at least, not without consulting me, because, Mikael, I know what I want and need, and I want and need *you*."

"You don't know me."

"I don't know who you were in the past. I never knew you as a boy or a young man, but I know who you are now. You're smart, courageous, honest. *Brave*. You have strong morals and values, and a fierce desire to do the right thing. I love that about you. In fact, I love you."

"You don't love me. You love the pleasure, you love the sensation."

"That's ridiculous!"

"It's not. I've seduced you with pleasure. I bonded you to me with all the hormones from sex and orgasm."

"Stop talking," she said, springing to her feet. "Your words are killing me. They're poisonous. Toxic. Just get rid of me now. Drop me off at the airport. But don't say another awful, hateful word."

He rose, towering over her. "You're being irrational."

"I am? Really? You spent eight days seducing me. Eight days making love to me in every conceivable position, showering me with gifts, assuring me that as your wife I'd be protected, safe, *secure*. Well, your idea of security is very different from mine, Sheikh Karim!"

"I'm sending you home to protect you."

"From what? *Whom*? The paparazzi? The media? The bloodthirsty public? Who are you protecting me from?"

"Me," he ground out, his voice low and hoarse.

She flung her head back, stared into his eyes, furious. "Maybe it's time you let go of the past, and your self-loathing and hatred. Maybe it's time to forgive. Because you are so determined to be fair to your country and your people but, Mikael Karim, you are not fair to yourself, and you're screwing up royally right now. You had me. You had my heart. And you've just thrown it all away."

They didn't speak on the walk back to the car.

They didn't speak, either, as the car traveled the long private driveway lined with hibiscus and palms to the enormous black and gold iron gates that marked the entrance to the Karim family's private beach.

The gates opened and then closed behind them. Jemma turned her head as if to get a last look at the brilliant blue coastline before it disappeared and swiftly wiped away a tear. The sun shone down on the water, and the ocean sparkled. She turned back to face the front, and wiped away another tear, seeing how the red gold sand stretched before them, reminding her of the Kasbah and the Bridal Palace and how Jemma and Mikael had spent the past eight days there.

All the experiences. The sensation. The pleasure. The emotion.

The car picked up speed on the empty highway. There was so little traffic in this part of Saidia that the driver could fly down the black ribbon of asphalt. He did, too.

Mikael stared out the window, lost in thought, and Jemma left him to his thoughts.

One minute all was quiet and the next they were smashed

sideways, slammed off the road in a screech of screaming brakes, screeching metal and shattering glass.

The impact knocked Mikael's car sideways, and the two cars, hit again, and once more, before the red sports car went sailing overhead to land off the road in the sand.

The heavy black sedan spun the opposite direction, until it finally crashed on the other side.

For a moment inside the car there was no sound.

Mikael shook his head, dazed.

"Jemma?" Mikael's hard voice cut through the stillness as he turned toward her.

She lay crumpled against the door, her face turned away from him.

"Jemma," he repeated more urgently, reaching for her, touching the side of her face. It was wet. He looked at his hand. It was covered in blood.

She was flown by helicopter to the royal hospital in Ketama. Mikael traveled with her, holding her hand. Mikael's chauffeur walked away with cuts and bruises like Mikael, while the driver of the other car didn't need a helicopter. He'd died at the scene.

Jemma spent hours in surgery as the doctors set bones and dealt with internal bleeding. She then spent the next few days heavily sedated.

Mikael refused to leave her side. Fortunately, he was the king, and this was the royal hospital named after the Karim family, so no one dared to tell him to leave her, either.

The doctors and specialists had all said she'd be okay. She was simply sedated to help reduce the swelling. She would mend better, and be in less pain, if she were sedated, and resting.

Mikael wanted her to rest, but he needed to know that she was okay.

So for three days he slept next to her bed. Nurses brought

coffee to him. His valet brought him clean clothes daily. Mikael used Jemma's hospital room shower when needed.

He struggled with that last day, the beach trip to Tagadir, her reaction when he told her he was sending her away, and then the silent car ride before the sports car slammed into them.

Was the accident karma?

Was this his fault, again?

He leaned over the bed, gently stroked her cheek, the bit of cheek he could reach between all the bandages. The shattered window had cut her head badly. They'd picked glass out for hours before finally getting the side of her head stitched and stapled closed.

He'd been furious that they shaved part of her hair, but the doctors insisted they had to. Now he just wanted to see her eyes open. He wanted to hear her voice. He needed to apologize and tell her he loved her and it wasn't lack of love that made him send her away, but the need to protect her, and do the right thing for her.

She didn't understand how much she meant to him. She was laughter and light and life.

She was his soul mate.

His other half, his better half. Yes, his queen.

That afternoon on the beach, she'd said hard things to him, but she'd also spoken the truth.

Mikael's battle wasn't with her. His battle was with himself.

He didn't like himself. Didn't love himself. Couldn't imagine her, her of all people, loving him.

And so he was sending her back to a world he wasn't part of, sending her to people who were more deserving.

Mikael closed his eyes, his fist pressed to his forehead, pushing against the thoughts and recriminations, as well as the memories tormenting him.

He should have been a better son to his mother. He should have denounced his father once he realized his father had lied, that his father had broken his promise to his mother. He should have given his mother the assistance, advice, and support she'd needed.

But he hadn't. And she'd died alone, in terrible emotional pain. And he couldn't forgive himself for his part in her suffering.

How could he?

He squeezed his fist tighter, pressed harder against his forehead, disgusted. Heartsick.

She'd be alive now if he'd given her help. She'd be alive if he'd acted when he should have. It would have been easy. Asking forgiveness was not that complicated. It was simply a matter of pride.

His eyes burned and he squeezed them shut, trying to hold the burning tears back. *Forgive me*, he thought, sending a silent prayer up to his mother.

And not that he deserved any help, or protection, but Jemma did. Jemma deserved so much, and maybe his mother could pull a few strings up there. Maybe his mother could do something on Jemma's behalf.

Help her, Mother. Help my Jemma. Help her heal, if you can.

And then gently, carefully he lifted Jemma's hands to his lips, pressed a kiss to her skin.

He didn't know how long he sat there, holding her hands, his lips pressed to her skin, but he wouldn't let her go. He refused to let her go. He needed her.

He loved her.

He couldn't be the man he wanted to be without her.

She had to survive and forgive him. She had to survive to be his friend, his lover, his companion. She had to survive so he could make things right with her.

"Forgive me, *laeela*," he whispered, exhausted by the vigil by her side, but not wanting to be anywhere else, either. He wouldn't leave her. Not now. Not ever.

Her eyes fluttered. Mikael sat forward. He stroked her brow, where her delicate, dark eyebrows arched. "Forgive me," he repeated. "I need you to come back. I need you with me."

"Forgive…" Jemma whispered, her eyes fluttering again, and slowly opening. Her brows tugged. Her gaze was unfocused. "Mikael?"

"You're awake."

"Where am I?"

"Ketama. The royal hospital."

"Why?"

"There was an accident." He stood, and gazed down intently into her eyes. "You were hurt."

It seemed hard for her to focus, but otherwise her eyes looked the same, clear and cool and green.

She blinked, and licked her lips, her mouth dry. "Do you have any water?"

"I'll ring the nurse." He pushed the button on the side of the bed. "Do you hurt?"

"A little. Not bad." She frowned. "I don't remember an accident."

"That's all right. You don't need to. It was bad. It's a miracle you're here."

She was silent a long moment. "What day is it?"

"Monday."

"No, what day? Of the eight days?"

He leaned over, kissed her gently on the cheek. "Day eleven, or twelve. I forget. It's been a blur."

"Oh." And then her expression changed, her brows knitting, tightening. "You're sending me home. You don't want me."

"Let's not talk about that right now."

"You don't love me."

"Jemma. *Laeela*," he said roughly, sounding agonized.

She turned her face away from him, closed her eyes. "It's fine. I want to go home. I want to go now."

A knot filled his throat. His chest ached with bottled emotion. "You can't go anywhere until you're better."

She tried to sit up. She winced at the effort.

"Lie down, be still—"

"I won't have you making decisions for me," she interrupted hoarsely. "I won't have you commanding me or dictating to me, because you're just like the others. You're just the same, making promises you never intended to keep—"

"That's not true," he interrupted fiercely, before lowering his voice. "I love you. I do. I don't know how it happened, but it happened. I didn't want a love match, but love found me anyway in you, and the only reason I was sending you home was to give you your freedom and future back."

"But my future is with you! My home is with you. And you, you—" She broke off and squeezed her eyes closed even as tears seeped beneath her lashes. "You don't even care."

"I care," he said, leaning over her, and kissing her carefully on the forehead, between bandages. "I care so much that I only want what's best for you, and I am not sure Saidia is best for you. It wasn't good for my mother. She was lonely here."

"But I'm not your mother," Jemma answered, opening her eyes. "And you're not your father. We can have our own marriage, and we can do it all differently. We can do it right. But you have to believe that, too. You have to fight for us, too."

"I'm fighting," he murmured, stroking her cheek gently, tenderly. She was all bruises, scrapes and stitches and more beautiful than any woman in the world. "I'm fighting for us, fighting for you. I haven't been able to leave your side, afraid that if I left, you'd disappear."

She struggled to smile even as tears fell, slipping from the corners of her eyes. "I'm here."

He smiled down at her, and caught a tear before it slid into her hair. "Yes, you are, my wife, my heart, my queen."

Jemma's lower lip trembled. "You can't ever threaten to send me away again."

"I won't. Not ever. We are going to make this work, and we will have hard days and arguments and hurt feelings, but

I promise you, I am here for you and with you. You and I are meant to be together."

"Not because it's your duty," she whispered.

He smiled. "No, it's not because of duty. We are together because you are my love, and the queen of my heart."

* * * * *

MILLS & BOON®
Hardback – March 2015

ROMANCE

The Taming of Xander Sterne	Carole Mortimer
In the Brazilian's Debt	Susan Stephens
At the Count's Bidding	Caitlin Crews
The Sheikh's Sinful Seduction	Dani Collins
The Real Romero	Cathy Williams
His Defiant Desert Queen	Jane Porter
Prince Nadir's Secret Heir	Michelle Conder
Princess's Secret Baby	Carol Marinelli
The Renegade Billionaire	Rebecca Winters
The Playboy of Rome	Jennifer Faye
Reunited with Her Italian Ex	Lucy Gordon
Her Knight in the Outback	Nikki Logan
Baby Twins to Bind Them	Carol Marinelli
The Firefighter to Heal Her Heart	Annie O'Neil
Thirty Days to Win His Wife	Andrea Laurence
Her Forbidden Cowboy	Charlene Sands
The Blackstone Heir	Dani Wade
After Hours with Her Ex	Maureen Child

MEDICAL

Tortured by Her Touch	Dianne Drake
It Happened in Vegas	Amy Ruttan
The Family She Needs	Sue MacKay
A Father for Poppy	Abigail Gordon